ABOUT THAT RULE

ABOUT THAT SERIES BOOK 2

ERIN LYNNE

BLURB

A vacation in Las Vegas with friends was going to be nothing but a good time.

When two of Samantha Nollins friends surprised everyone that they eloped, she was ready to party. After all, she was known to celebrate at all times, along with her bestie Nate Haddic. However, when they wake up the next day, their two friends weren't the only ones who eloped!

Samantha and Nate immediately go to the court house, only to be told they need to wait ninety-days and try to make their marriage work.

There was nothing worse than two players who had to settle down. In order to keep their friendship intact, the created rules – which seemed easy enough.

First rule, no sex. This was a bummer, but there was no way they were cheating on each other, even if the wedding was fake.

Second, they had to visit each other more, which was no sweat of their backs.

Third, they couldn't tell anyone. This was mainly because it was only ninety-days, why get anyone else involved?

Fourth was more because of the court order, but they had to take pictures of them together. This way, they could show the judge they tried, but it didn't work.

Lastly, the most important role, was no falling for each other.

But, what happens if the lines start to blur?

About That Rule

Copyright © 2022 Erin Lynne

All rights reserved. No part of this book may be reproduced in any form or transmitted in any form including electronic or mechanical means, without permission in writing from the publisher, except by a reviewer who may quote brief passages in a review or critical articles.

This book is a work of fiction. Names, characters, places, and incidents either are the product of the author's imagination or are used fictitiously. Any resemblance to actual persons, living or dead, events, or locales is entirely coincidental.

This book is licensed for your personal enjoyment only. Thank you for respecting the author's work.

Published: Erin Lynne 2022

Editing: Word Nerd Editing

Cover Design: ebook Cover Designs

Formatting: Yours Truly Book Services

ISBN:

DEDICATION

To the two girls who've been my besties for as long as I can remember. Senior Dixie and Sensible Saltz, we went from being neighbors in the Christiana Hood, recitals at Stage Lights, to bar crawls that ended at Cleatus's apartment. I am so lucky to have you two in my life, from childhood to now. Adrienne and Deanna, thanks for always being there for me, in the good and not so great, and supporting me all the way (chalk houses and Oscars to the college parties and now raising kids). I love you two like crazy. xo

CHAPTER 1

"HOLY HANGOVER, BATMAN," Samantha Nollins mumbled to her friends as she slinked into an empty chair at the table. There was so much noise in the restaurant, it made her wince with the headache she was fighting off. She pushed her sunglasses closer to her face as if they would protect her from the raging pounding in her head. Even though they were seated inside, all the light was attacking her massive hangover. Everything was way too bright, too loud, and just too much. Oddly, she wanted to smile, but had no energy. This hangover was a reminder she'd done Las Vegas proud.

Her twin brother, Noah, handed her a bottle of water and some aspirin, prepared to nurse her back to health. He had always been the more responsible one. "I told you to stop taking all those shots."

"Very sacrilegious of you to even say those words while we are vacationing in Sin City," she said, her voice barely above a whisper over the slot machines and music surrounding them. "It was my duty to party. I had to pick up your slack. You're welcome."

"We're thirty and on family vacation." He shot her a

pointed look, not cutting her any slack, per usual. "This wasn't some giant party from our twenties."

Every year, her parents planned a huge vacation for them and four other families. It was a pact her mom made with her college best friends to make sure, no matter where life took them, they saw each other annually. Samantha and Noah grew up with these other families, and while they weren't blood related, they all were thick as thieves.

Elena Bianchi, who sat next to Noah, shook her head as if she didn't agree with Samantha. "I knew you were going to feel like crap the moment you drank straight from the champagne bottle, screaming how happy you were for Rafe and Charlotte."

Despite feeling like shit, this did force a smile from Samantha. Rafe, Elena's older brother, and Charlotte, who had also grown up with them because of their parents, had taken Vegas to the next level last night. They'd showed up late to dinner, then shocked the shit out of everyone. After years and years of fighting, they'd arrived with rings on their fingers.

That was right. Rings on fingers, people.

They'd done something Samantha would never, ever consider.

Ugh.

They got married.

She had nothing against matrimony for people who believed in it, but it still made her cringe. It seemed like a waste to make such a big commitment so young. Sure, they were in their thirties, but still. Marriage wasn't in the cards for Samantha unless it was an end to a means. Like, her getting married was the only way to save earth from an alien invasion type shit.

"What are you thinking about that made you so quiet?" Gabriella, Elena and Rafe's other sibling, asked.

"Alien invasion," she answered with a smirk.

Noah gave her a high five. "I don't even care what made you think of aliens, I'm just impressed."

"Honest, I was thinking about marriage. Either way, I was buying shots and ordering champagne and partying my ass off because Rafe and Charlotte got married. Rafe pulled a damn Beyonce and put a ring on it. Do you guys get that? After all these years of us begging them to stop fighting, they got married! While it isn't for me, we've been watching them play cat and mouse forever. If nothing else, I was celebrating them not arguing all the time anymore."

Everyone seemed to agree with this sentiment. Another person joined them at the table who seemed way too not hungover for Samantha's liking. Jason Madison, Charlotte's older brother, stretched out his legs as he got comfortable sitting next to Samantha. "How's everyone feeling this morning?"

"Like death," Samantha sulked. "I hate how cheerful you sound. How are you not hungover?"

He gave a cat-like grin, like raging until four in the morning was the norm for him. "There is a method to my madness. I drink water after every drink. And before I go to bed, I down even more water and take two Advil. Probably fucks with my liver, but it works."

"You two were wild last night," Elena told them with a giggle. "Well, you guys and Nate. I left before you all went to the club at the Paris hotel. You were talking about how you planned to party all night. I'm pretty sure there was mention of who could take the most shots. And there was something about having a dance-off because all three of you drunk fools declared yourselves the best dancer."

"I can't believe you're questioning who was the best dancer. It's me, obviously," Samantha said, even though she wanted to crawl under the table.

Jason shrugged like he had no care in the world. "I should have been partying like crazy. You all heard the news. My sister got married—and to Rafe, of all people. It was celebratory. Shocking, but celebratory."

Samantha rested her head on his shoulder. "I tried to explain that, but they were too focused on my hangover."

"They're jealous because they all went to bed like they had work today. Which is ridiculous. We're in Vegas for fuck's sake. But, I have to admit, I was only at the club for, like, ten minutes. You and Nate were planning to rage until they kicked you out." Jason stopped talking when his phone vibrated. After he read the text, he groaned.

"Who is it?" Gabriella asked, taking a bite of her omelet.

"Remind me to never give my number to a one-night stand again."

Samantha downed her water, shocked he needed the reminder. "How did you make such a rookie mistake?"

"All the booze we inhaled last night. There are some fuzzy parts, but I didn't stay at the club long because I left with Sarah. I think that was her name."

"How do you not know her name?" Elena cringed with disgust. She'd been in a relationship with this guy named Sam for a while, and he was such a dud. But playing the field was nonsense to her. Samantha wished her friend would live a little and enjoy being young. She was one step about from being hitched like Charlotte and Rafe.

His gaze went to his phone, which made him smile again. "I'm sure she told me at some point, but I forget. Her text...well, it was visual, if you know what I mean. It wasn't like her name was displayed anywhere."

Gabriella pretended to gag. "So gross."

"Why did you give her your number?" Samantha wasn't as prudish as her friends. She didn't wince at one-night stands and loved playing the field.

"The sex was insane, so when she asked for my number, I gave it to her out of pure orgasmic exhaustion. Besides, we leave tomorrow, who's going to kick a gift horse in the mouth, you know? One more fuck won't hurt."

Elena scrunched up her nose, still repulsed by him. "Not only is that disgusting, but you didn't even get the saying right."

Jason grabbed a rogue mimosa and took a sip. He put the glass down and tilted his head at her. "I always use a condom, so it's not disgusting. And, on the bright side, I get vacation sex one more day, so I shouldn't have bitched about the text. Sammy, what did you and Nate do after I left? You were slamming drinks and dancing like crazy."

Samantha put her head on the table and groaned. "I barely remember you leaving. In fact, I don't remember much after Elena and the rest of the party poopers left."

Noah nudged his sister. "I'm not a party pooper. I have training as soon as I get home. There's no break for me before soccer season starts. I need to stay hydrated and healthy, not hungover and exhausted. It will be brutal if I'm not prepared."

"Brutal, but worth it," Jason said, way too much happiness in his voice.

It had to be from the sex.

Samantha, on the other hand, needed to drink as much water as possible so she was up for round two of celebrating. It was the last day of vacation. She wanted to cram in one more night of getting wild into this trip. It wasn't going to happen if she felt like shit.

NATE ROLLED OVER and his stomach debated throwing up. Hangovers were a different beast once he hit thirty. Now that he was thirty-one, his body was revolting against him. He swore his liver put him on probation from his partying last night.

Not that he had any regrets.

This hangover was worth it though because...well, he was in Vegas. That, and last night, he celebrated the news of his two friends eloping. Such an epic move he never expected from Rafe and Charlotte. Like usual, though, it was just Sammy and him still at the bar having fun by the end of the night. In their group, they were always the ones who stayed out way too late, having way too much fun. Since they were kids, they had been ready to cause trouble.

Last night was no exception. It was blurry what happened after Jason left the bar with some woman he met while dancing. He vaguely recalled getting in and out of cabs and laughing with Sammy when she pulled a bottle of champagne out of her purse.

Women and their purses. It was like a bag full of surprises. When she showed him the bottle of Chandon she had stashed in her purse, which she said was for emergencies, a handful of pens, pepper spray, and a pack of gum fell out. It was like watching Mary Poppins search through her bag. He bet she had aspirin in there, which he could use.

Fuck this hangover.

When he rolled over, paper crumbled beneath him. He squinted at the receipt. He'd ordered a pizza. No surprise there. He was always hungry when he drank too much. Even though it had been a while since he'd been as drunk as he was last night, old faithful pizza showed its face.

He pulled the sheets over his head to block the sun from shining in. There had to be a way for him to get more sleep. According to the pizza receipt, there was a strong possibility he hadn't gotten back to his room until four a.m.

Today was the last full day of vacation. Staying in bed sounded like a waste, even if his body was begging for hydration and sleep. But if Samantha and Jason weren't moping in their hotel rooms, he had no excuse to lay around. Grabbing his phone, he texted Samantha.

Tell me you didn't get out of bed.

Her text back was almost immediate. It was only a picture of her, and it made him chuckle. Not that she was funny looking or anything. Actually, if Nate hadn't grown up with her, he would have been the first to admit how hot she was. Even if she was struggling in the current text.

Her long, dark brown hair was thrown into a sloppy ponytail with strands of hair sticking up everywhere, and her dark brown eyes were covered with sunglasses. Samantha was someone with a perpetual smile on her face, but in the text, she was frowning. To top it off, she was in her wrinkled dress from last night.

Another text vibrated in from her.

If I made it out, you better too.

Not the response he'd been hoping for. He crawled out of bed to get ready, figuring food would help his current state. After he showered, brushed his teeth, and got dressed, he sat on the bed, debating whether he should just go back to sleep. Guilt set in. He didn't get to see this group of friends often since he lived in New York and they resided in California where they'd all grown up. His phone went off again.

You better get down here. I can't be the only hungover mess.

So much for more of the elusive sleep.

Nate took a quick selfie of how miserable he looked and sent it back to Sammy. She would get a kick out of it. He went to delete the picture and saw some from the night before. These snapshots should have been funny.

Swipe after swipe, his night was pieced together.

And it was not looking good.

SEARCHING THE HOTEL room, there was nothing—not one single piece of evidence to confirm what seemed likely to have happened based on the pictures. His hangover was actually better than the anxiety pulsing through him. He took a deep breath. His imagination was getting the better of him. If Samantha wasn't freaking out, he wasn't going to freak out.

There was nothing to worry about.

All he had to do was see Samantha, then they'd laugh it off.

With much more pep in his step than he'd had earlier, he got in the elevator and made it to where his friends were for brunch in ten minutes. All their parents were on a tour of the Hoover Dam, so it was, as his mom, Natalie, put it, "just the kids" spending time together.

"Look who made it," Elena joked when he joined the table. Everyone was there, except Charlotte and Rafe. No one had seen them leave their hotel room since their marriage announcement.

Maybe there was one reason to get married.

He almost gagged.

Marriage was not for him. Not even if there was sex on the regular. He could get that now without having to be a husband or have a wife.

"Thank god you look like shit," Samantha mumbled, patting the chair next to her so he could sit down.

That Samantha's biggest concern was having a partner in crime for their shared hangover was reassuring. There were no signs of *what the hell did we do last night*—which was promising. Nothing seemed wrong other than their previous alcohol consumption. Nate let out a breath of relief. There wasn't any awkwardness either.

Everything was fine.

When he showed her the pictures from last night, they would laugh about it. She probably had pictures on her phone too. Nothing was wrong.

"What did you guys do after I left last night?" Jason asked, having the nerve to drink a mimosa. How he managed his lifestyle was beyond Nate.

"Just partied." He kept it brief. A small, minuscule part of him still wanted to talk to Samantha before laughing off what happened. He couldn't shake that last night was a bigger problem than he was giving credit.

No one badgered him for more details as everyone made plans for the rest of the day. Slowly, everyone started to leave. Elena and Gabriella went shopping to find a unique wedding gift. Noah, the ever-dedicated soccer player, went to the gym. After texting with a stupid grin on his face, Jason left.

"And then there were two," Samantha said. Empty water glasses were littered around her on the table. "I swear, if Oliver surprises everyone and shows up for vacation, I'm not celebrating. I know it's been years since we've seen him, but I can't handle another drink right now."

Oliver Bolton was the last member of their pack. He was the eldest at thirty-six and had lived in London since college. He'd been supposed to make an appearance for this trip, but something with work came up.

"Did you have fun last night?" Nate treaded lightly. Like he was nervous about her response. Like maybe his gut reaction was right. Like last night changed things.

She gave him a small smile. "From what I can remember, last night was wild."

Fuck.

She didn't remember everything either.

"Wild—good wording."

"Why are you acting weird?"

Nate was going to try another approach. "Have you looked through any of the pictures from last night?"

Samantha let out a small chuckle. "Why, are they posted all over the internet or something?"

Shit, he hoped not.

"No, on your phone. Do you have pictures on your phone from last night?" He spelled it out for her. His efforts to get her to look at the pictures, if she hadn't already, was exhausting.

She shook her head. "I've used my phone three times today—and all were to text you. Looking at my screen hurts. I can't party like I used to."

Looking at his screen hurt too, but for completely different reasons.

"Do me a solid and look through your phone. Tell me if you have pictures from last night. I don't remember everything either, but maybe we can piece together a story."

She huffed but grabbed her phone and started swiping through. When her jaw dropped, it was the first sign things were as bad as he'd anticipated. When she muttered, "Fuck," it confirmed it.

"Nate, what the hell?" Her voice didn't sound as exhausted now. She was on edge, just like him.

"Maybe we did it as a joke. Like, let's just take pictures to be funny because of Rafe and Charlotte."

Samantha took a deep breath. Her leg started to shake under the table. "Maybe."

Neither one of them spoke, but Nate guessed they were both thinking the same thing.

Who the hell got married as a joke?

CHAPTER 2

THERE WAS ONLY one way to validate what had happened. Her hangover was a ghost of the past. She had more pressing issues to deal with. Like figuring out if she was actually married.

She winced.

Who wanted to be married at thirty? Forty, maybe, but thirty was way too young. This was no reflection of Nate. If they hadn't grown up together, she would have been all over him. He was gorgeous, with thick dark hair that reminded her of Jon Snow's shaggy look from *Game of Thrones*. If he let it grow out just a little bit longer, his hair would be ready for a man bun. His eyes were dark blue, almost more of a gray. His toned body wasn't from the gym, but from his career. Nate remodeled houses. He didn't just tell his team what to do, either, but worked on each home right along with them. There was something sexy about a man who knew how to use his hands.

Now wasn't the time for counting off all Nate's hotness. There was a possibility he might be her husband. If that was the case, they needed to get this shit annulled ASAP.

"We don't qualify for the void option for annulment." Nate informed her. Somebody had done his research. It was reassuring he wasn't living in la-la-land and hoped they'd live in marital bliss. There was no way that was happening. "We might be able to get the annulment since we were under the influence. It would qualify of not being in right state of mind."

"This seems pretty standard given we were beyond wrecked when we got married. Besides, this is Vegas. I'm sure annulling marriage is a daily thing. All we have to do is go to the courthouse and file the required paperwork. Then, in twenty-one days, marriage annulled." Samantha scrolled through the article on her phone to make sure she didn't miss anything. It only took a quick Google search of *got married in Vegas and don't want to be married* to find a million links.

Her marriage was easy come, easy go. She was just another hungover person looking for a way to get a quicky divorce.

She didn't want to get married, but it did seem a little insensitive to the constitution of it all. Part of her felt guilty. There were people like her parents—ugh, people like Charlotte and Rafe—who truly believed their partnership was for the long haul. Samantha getting married and divorced within twenty-four hours was bad. Even for her and all her wildness.

"Come on. Uber is here." Nate grabbed her elbow and guided her to get in the car.

"It's weird to see you so business-like," she said, scooting over for him to join her.

He sat next to her, and the car took off. "Because we get to see each other for vacations, parties, or when one of us is visiting the other. It's all for fun. This is far from fun. We might be fucking married." His voice sounded pained.

The message was heard loud and clear: being married was not fun. She agreed, but he didn't have to be such a meanie about it.

The first place they went was Paradise Wedding Chapel. They both had pictures of them basically dry humping in front of the building. It was a good thing neither of them remembered kissing—there was a sneaking suspicion it might've been a game changer. There were more pictures of them inside with the officiant, in what appeared to be a wedding ceremony.

They spoke to the woman at the front desk, asking for her to provide some detail on what happened the night before. It took all of three minutes for the chapel to provide the paperwork to confirm they had, indeed, gotten married.

Neither of them spoke while they waited outside for another Uber. Just like they didn't speak on the drive to the courthouse. Samantha was overwhelmed with guilt, but she figured it was normal. Last night, two people she adored got married because they were in love. Drunk Samantha had probably wanted the same thing they shared.

Sober Samantha did not want marriage.

There was no way sober Nate wanted it either. The two of them were way too similar with relationships. They were notoriously single and loved the life of not being committed to anyone. Neither of them invested in anything more than a casual hook up. They always joked with each other about who was the bigger flirt because commitment wasn't their thing. Granted, getting married was as serious as it got, but their hoax wedding wasn't the best example.

Arriving at the courthouse, Nate held his hand out to help her get out of the car.

"Careful," she told him once she stood next to him. "The judge might see this and think we're the real thing. Our annulment will fly out the window."

He groaned, looking up at the sky. "Fuck, could you imagine?"

"I'm trying not to take this personal," she responded to his continuous bad attitude, giving him a light shove toward the entry doors. "You're treating me like this is doom's day."

They walked into the building and waited in line. There were at least ten people ahead of them. She wondered what they were here for. There was no way all these people needed to annul their intoxicated vows. That would be insane.

But...it was Vegas.

"Don't take it personal. I'm sure if we hadn't grown up together, we already would've fucked. You don't need me to tell you how hot you are. But commitment for the rest of my life? I don't think I'm cut out for that—not with anyone."

They probably would have had sex. Hot, sweaty, intense sex. Samantha and Nate would ruin each other for anyone else. If they ever crossed that line, she just had this feeling there would be no going back. Better for her to keep Nate compartmentalized in the friendship box.

As his friend, she needed to dig deeper on why a wife was never on the horizon for him. She always figured he'd get sick of the single life at some point. Most people do. "Never? You don't think you would find a partner?"

He shrugged as they took a few steps forward. The line was moving, so there was a silver lining.

"Why?" Samantha asked.

He turned to look at her. "I get bored easily with women. Even when I've dated, after a month or two, I'm over it. It's been like that since I was fifteen. That's sixteen years of dating, sleeping around, having girlfriends—you name it. I've never wanted to stick it out with one person. I enjoy being single. I like my lifestyle, you know?"

She nodded. More than ever, she understood being single and loving it.

"Next!" a woman called.

It was their turn.

"We need an annulment." Nate didn't beat around the bush.

Samantha pushed the paperwork they'd filled out. "Here are all our documents."

The woman behind the desk rolled her eyes, typing their

information into her computer. "Have a seat. I will call your name when the judge is ready to see you."

With nothing else to do but wait, Samantha and Nate found two empty chairs in the lobby and sat down.

WHAT A FUCKING mess.

Nate was living his nightmare. He had no intension of ever getting married, let alone to a deep-rooted family friend. If shit hit the fan, their families would be impacted. This annulment needed to happen—like right after they said *I do*. What had they been thinking, to actually get married?

"I'm losing my sanity sitting here," Samantha confessed, fidgeting next to him. "Want to play a game or something?"

A game would pass the time. Who knew how long they'd be waiting? Samantha was smart and texted their family and friends, telling everyone they were doing a tour today and would be back for dinner. Since everyone else was busy having fun in Vegas and not annulling a marriage, no one asked any questions about their supposed tour. Which, in hindsight, was lucky for them. The less people involved, the better.

"Sure, do you have one on your phone?"

"I'm no amateur. Of course I have games on my phone."

This wasn't a surprise. Samantha was fun, wild, and carefree. Games on her phone were probably to keep her entertained at all times. She was hardly without a smile.

"We can play Heads Up, Hang Man, Would You Rather, Five Second Guess—"

"How many games do you have?" he interrupted her. It was amazing her phone had enough storage for her entertainment needs.

"Or Do You Know Me. These are the games I can play with two or more people. I left out the ones that are one-player only."

He had a much-needed laugh at her silliness. "Why? Why do you have that many games on your phone?"

"I'm responsible for the ice breaker at our monthly meeting. Everyone loves a good giggle before we have to listen to metrics on advertising, ways to increase sales, and gaining a new audience." She was a Social Media Director for one of the largest credit card companies in the country, and only she could make someone smile during the busy days at work.

"What's your excuse for the one-player games?"

"Wouldn't you like to know," she teased back.

"You shouldn't keep secrets from your husband."

Their easy banter immediately stopped.

Nate showed her the smile that always got him out of trouble. "Husband jokes too soon?"

"Yes. Until the ink is dried on our annulment papers, husband jokes are too soon."

"Let's play one of your games. Which one is somber like our mood?" he goaded her.

Her smile came back. "The Do You Know Me game. Ask, and you shall receive. Should we do the questions suitable for all ages or adults only?"

"The whole reason we're in the waiting room is because of an adult decision. Let's play those questions."

She rubbed her hands together as if she had a devious plan. "This is right up my alley."

Other than her random giggle, it was quiet for a few minutes while she typed away on her phone then handed it to him. "You need to write what you think my answers are."

Easy instructions and no talk of marriage. There was no way he could screw this up.

Until he read the first question.

What is my favorite sexual position?

The idea of a naked Samantha riding him invaded his imagination. He bet her athletic body was drool-worthy when she took her clothes off. It had been a while since he'd seen her in a bathing suit, but fuck. Samantha had nice boobs that looked like the perfect handful, and her pale, creamy skin would be tinted pink from his stubble after he ravaged her.

Shit, he was getting hard. He shifted in his seat to hide his growing erection. His dick was hard in a fucking courthouse. He needed to get his shit together.

"This is taking you too long. I'll give you a freebie. The first answer is Reverse Cowgirl. It's the only way I get off. Wait—that's a lie. Me on top is the only way I get off."

Information overload.

Samantha wasn't doing his hard dick any favors. Nate wondered why it was taking so long for the judge to see them. There was no way he could take this quiz about Samantha and her sexual preferences. His whole life, he'd managed to keep her in the friend-zone. Well...outside the whole married thing. Talking to her about sex might make him realize how badly he wanted her.

Sex with her.

Not anything else.

They couldn't cross that line.

He gave her back the phone. "Let's play something else."

"Wimp," she mocked, then flipped through her phone. "How about Heads Up?"

"Samantha Nollins and Nathan Haddic, you're next."

The hallway they walked down to get to the judge's chamber was sterile. No pictures, just whitewashed cement walls taunting him of all the bad decisions that had led him to this moment. They stepped into a room smaller than he expected for a court room. The judge sat on a raised table, with a court reporter a few seats down and a bailiff standing in front of the bench.

The bailiff announced, "Honorable Judge Harold Shunton

preceding. Samantha Nollins and Nathan Haddic are here to annul their marriage."

The judge glared down at them through his bifocal glasses.

"Quickie wedding in Vegas, I presume." Even his tone was dismissive, like this had been a long day for him and their annulment was the straw that broke the camel's back. The hope of an uncomplicated annulment was flittering away.

"Yes, sir," Samantha solidly answered.

Judge Shunton's dark eyes shifted between them. "How long have you two known each other?"

"My whole life." Her voice shook as she responded, sounding less confident than she had a minute ago.

"Interesting," the judge told them, shifting through their paperwork. "You two have known each other your whole lives but are quick to annul your union. Why is that?"

Silence resided over them. Nate doubted the man sitting in front of him would appreciate they wanted an annulment because they both liked causal sex—with other people—and a marriage would ruin that.

"An answer?" the judge demanded.

"We've known each other our whole lives," Samantha started, then clamped her mouth shut, realizing that fact wasn't helping their case.

"As you've previously stated." The judge narrowed his eyes.

Nate rubbed her back so she knew he would take over. "And since we've known each other for so long, we're better friends. We've always known that."

"Right," she affirmed with a nod of her head.

The judge took off his glasses to rub his eyes and then shoved them back on. "If you've always known you were better off as friends, why did you get married in the first place?"

"Good question," Nate said, not as patient as he'd been. "We'd had a lot to drink."

The judge crossed his arms.

"Because our two friends had just eloped and we were all celebrating," Nate quickly added.

"Yes," Samantha interjected to sway the judge. "It was a happy moment for everyone. We went out, danced, took pictures, drank champagne—it was a night all about love."

"We indulged too much because of their marriage. This morning, after seeing the pictures on our phones and realizing what we'd done while in an intoxicated state, we came here to annul what had happened." Nate didn't understand why there were so many questions. Wasn't it enough they didn't want to be married?

"May I see the pictures?" the judge asked.

"Yes, sir," they both answered, then stepped to the bailiff and handed her their phones. The judge analyzed each picture before giving their phones back.

"I see this happen too often. It's nauseating the way people reject a loving partner."

Oh, shit. This was bad.

"Your request for an annulment is *not* granted. You two need to learn a valuable lesson, which I think will turn out to be exactly what you need. Try to make this marriage work. Spend time together, be faithful, learn about your partner and yourself. If in ninety days you still want the annulment, we can revisit. The verdict may change only if I see you gave it your all and you still don't want to be married. Let's see how the ninety days go." He slammed his gavel down and exited the court room, leaving Nate and Samantha with their jaws hanging open.

THIS WAS THE WORST case scenario. They could probably get an attorney and repeal the decision, but she was sure that would require more of her time in Vegas. And that wasn't even considering the money for the legal fees or the hassle that appealing could take longer than the ninety days the judge demanded of them. She wasn't sure what the better option was: being tied up in court or marriage—and not the fun kind of tied up.

Both made her shudder.

Both were like a prison sentence.

Both didn't give an immediate solution.

"What are we going to do?" Nate sounded numb, which she understood. This had been a surreal experience. "I don't want to be married. Ever."

She sensed a major breakdown approaching. Whether it would be from him or her was up in the air. This was a disaster. The two infamous singletons were now married to each other.

"We can't freak out." Samantha wasn't sure if she was selling this advice to herself or Nate.

For the past hour since they'd left the courthouse, they'd been sitting in front of the Bellagio fountain in silence. Everyone around them was enjoying Las Vegas while they were in mourning of their old, single status. She wished she'd packed something black to wear to pair with her gloomy mood.

"I'm trying to remain calm." There was an edge to his voice she wasn't used to be on the receiving end of. "But I recently found out I'm married to a childhood friend, a judge refused to annul said marriage, and now I have to put effort into this fucking union, even if I don't want to."

"Hey, we're both in the same boat, don't give me an attitude," she sassed him right back.

His head dropped to his hands. "You're right. I'm sorry. What are we going to do?"

Samantha scooted closer to him and rested her head on his shoulder. "We're going to continue living our lives and just see more of each other over the next three months. We'll take pictures for proof of how we spent time together. We come back to Vegas in ninety days and show the judge we tried, then we get our annulment."

He lifted his head to look at her. "Wouldn't it be quicker to appeal the decision?"

"When I Googled it, it said it could take a month, but often, it lasts longer. Some have quoted years. It just seems easier to go along with the judgment and come back."

"Fuck."

"Exactly. We can do this our way, though. It'll be the only way we survive the next ninety days."

"I live in New York. You live in California," he muttered.

"We already visit each other. It'll just be more frequent now. Who cares? We always have a good time together."

"He said we have to be faithful. I've never been in a serious relationship and now I can't have sex for ninety days."

Samantha laughed. "Think of this as a good workout for your arm muscles. It's not like I'll be having sex either. This will just be a really long dry spell. If it means we won't be married in ninety days, I can do it. Let's try to be positive and not let this decision ruin our lives."

She was proud of her positivity. Even though she was dreading the next three months, at least she had Nate to complain to. They could do this. It wasn't like they were married for real.

CHAPTER 3

WHEN NATE CAME home from Las Vegas, his mood didn't improve. He still couldn't get over the fact that he'd gotten married. What the fuck had he been thinking? If nothing else, at least he was married to someone who understood him and was on the same level when it came to relationships. He and Samantha had been friends for so long, even though they lived across the country from each other, they constantly talked. Whether it was through their frequent emails, a text of something funny, or a random drunk dial, they'd stayed connected over the years.

Sexy, funny, and smart was the best way to describe her.

Samantha was the total package. But she was only a friend. His partner in crime. He couldn't count the number of times they'd played wingman for the other. She was the female version of himself when it came to dating.

The irony of two heartbreakers being married to each other hadn't gone unnoticed.

In fact, if he wasn't the one stuck in a commitment, he would've found their situation hilarious. But he was married. And it was not funny.

His phone rang. It was Samantha.

"Hey," he answered, slouching down on his couch. She let out a small giggle, which was confusing. Nothing was funny to him. "How are you laughing right now?"

"Because I refuse to let this whole husband and wife thing ruin my attitude. I figured you're about to go bananas, so I'm here to tell you it's nowhere near as bad as you think. You'll get to see more of my pretty face, how awful could that be?"

She had a valid point. Samantha did have a pretty face. "Outside of the whole celibacy thing, not bad at all," he responded.

"It's only a few months. You can manage."

"Can you?" Curiosity set in as he sat up.

"These won't be my favorite three months, but I can do it. Neither of us want to be married, but that doesn't mean I'll make a mockery out of the institution of it all."

"Yeah, I agree. And it seems sleazy to cheat on you, even though, it isn't like real cheating."

Ever since the ruling, the thought of sleeping with someone else while he was married to Samantha seemed wrong. It was Sammy. She didn't deserve to have someone, real or fake, not be faithful to her.

"Only two days into our marriage and you've turned into such a romantic. Your words are so sentimental." Her voice was filled with sarcasm.

This made him chuckle. "I didn't know you wanted romance, Sammy."

"Romance always seems manufactured to me. I want something real, not pretty words because you think you have to say them."

"Well, I promise to never tell you something because I think it's what you need to hear."

"Same."

"Thanks for calling. I was on the verge of losing my shit over this."

"Somehow, I knew that," she said in a soothing voice. "Do you think we should set up some…I don't know, some rules? This is new territory, and I don't want either of us to end up scathed."

Seemed simple enough. "That makes sense."

He heard her shuffle around, probably getting comfortable. "Our first rule is obvious: we're on a sexual hiatus until this contract is annulled."

"Ugh," he groaned. No sex for three months was brutal. He was the king of random hook-ups. This would be the longest he'd gone without sex since…well, since he started having sex.

"I feel the same way, but it's not like we can't flirt with other people. I guess kissing would be okay too, we just can't do anything naked."

"I'm going to have the worst case of blue balls."

"Don't be so dramatic."

"I'm not a monk."

"I'm not either. I wonder what the female version of a monk is called?"

"Monachos," he informed her quickly.

"How do you know that?"

"I like Jeopardy. It was one of the answers that stuck with me."

She made a humming noise. "Maybe because it sounds like food. You always did like nachos."

Her comment made him crack a smile.

"Back to the rules." She sounded like she was on a mission. "Rule number two: we need to schedule frequent visits. I love New York, so really, this is a benefit for me. Once a month, I'll fly out to visit you for a weekend."

"I'll do the same and come see you. I make my own schedule, so I can stay a week at a time. My mom and Mark will be happy to see me so much, but it will bring on a shit load of questions. What are we telling people?"

The always chatty Samantha paused. "I didn't think of that. With Charlotte and Rafe getting hitched, if we tell our parents we got wasted and married each other, they'll be disappointed. Either that or they'll think we're next to actually settle down. Is there any way you can tell them you're visiting because you're looking at remodeling and flipping houses in California?"

"That isn't far from the truth. I can kill two birds with one stone. I've been thinking of expanding business to the west coast anyway."

"Really?" she responded with surprise.

It was happening to him again. There'd been this nagging feeling something was off in his life, and it had been around for months. No amount of business success, one-night stands, or time with his family had fixed the ache. Like something was missing from his life.

No, he dismissed the idea. He had everything he needed.

"Just like you, I love New York, but the market in California is insane. I could flip houses faster out there."

"Would that require you to move back?"

"Technically, no. I could travel back and forth. Have multiple jobs at once with a foreman leading and do more oversight than all the grit work, which has always been my goal."

"You'll get there. Ever since we were kids, you were always building something. I have so many memories of you remodeling my Lego masterpieces because you didn't like them."

There was no doubt she was smiling. All his life, she had consistently been one of his biggest cheerleaders. Having her around more in these next three months was bound to put him in a better mood, even with all the stress from work.

"Okay, back to the rules. Rule number three: we don't tell anyone what's going on. I don't think people would even bat an eye to us hanging out more often. Whenever you visit, we always grab drinks, so it will just be more of the same."

"Agreed." This situation, outside of no sex, wasn't that bad. Spending time with Samantha was no sweat off his back.

"Remember, though, you need to romance me. This can't be the obligatory beer catch up. We need to go out on dates and take cute pictures together. We need to show the judge we tried, but in the end, it didn't work because we're better off as friends. Rule number four: we have to do some couple-y crap every visit," Samantha reminded him.

"Fine," he rushed out, ready to end talking about this damn marriage. "The final rule, the mother of all rules—under no circumstances do we confuse what's happening. This is all fake. Neither of us can get caught up in the romance of this."

Nate had no misconception he was going to fall in love. However, he needed to guarantee Samantha didn't blur the lines. He refused to lose her as a friend because she thought a kiss on the cheek meant more than a picture for an annulment.

"I'll be laughing so hard at your lame attempt to be romantic, I won't have time to be conflicted."

"Oh, shut up," he responded jokingly to her snub.

"The last thing I want is a relationship, let alone with you. I promise, these next three months are going to fly by. Before we know it, you'll be banging all of New York again."

As always, her attitude made him smile. When they got off the phone, he felt significantly better. One day, Samantha was going to be a great wife. Just not for him.

DAY FOUR OF marriage, and it hadn't been too excruciating. Sure, Samantha still felt like an ass for walking down the Vegas aisle for no good reason, but it wasn't like anyone was aware of it. She cringed at the rules she and Nate had made for the next three months. It was like they were playing Survivor, but their version was to stay faithful.

Pitiful, right?

"Sammy, what's wrong?" Becca, someone who doubled as a work colleague and best friend, asked while tapping the table to get her attention during happy hour.

She gave a fake smile, as if all was well, as a response. The bar buzzed with chatter, but she heard her friend loud and clear.

Becca wasn't having it. "Seriously, girl. You just got home from Vegas and haven't told any inappropriate dick stories. I was expecting some rendition of wild sex with some guy who looked like one of the hotties from Magic Mike. Or a crazy story of public nudity. Instead, all you said was the trip was fun and Charlotte and Rafe got married."

Those weren't the only nuptials last week, but Becca had no clue.

"Wait..." Becca's brown eyes widened. "Is that why you're off? Did seeing two of your close friends getting married wig you out? I know you don't like commitment, but this is a bit extreme. Even for you."

Samantha picked up her beer and chugged the remainder of it. Drinks were supposed to be fun, not a reminder of her current marital status. She was curious if Nate was having the same issue.

"Seriously, what's wrong?"

She pulled out her wallet and put a twenty on the table to cover her drink and tip. Once this stupid marriage was over, she was throwing herself a damn party. Open bar and everything. "Nothing is wrong. I'm tired from playing catch up with work since I got home."

"If you don't come back to work on Monday with your chipper attitude, I'll continue to annoy you about whatever's going on with you. It seems like Vegas was so much fun, you're trying to keep it a secret. You know I'll badger you until you tell me every yummy detail about whoever is keeping you quiet." Becca raised her eyebrows in warning.

No way was this secret ever coming out. Samantha said goodbye to everyone at the table and left. She supposed this was what Friday nights were like when you were married.

Lame.

CHAPTER 4

WEEKENDS WERE NOT going to be a good time if they continued having repeats of last night. Samantha had a whole new appreciation for the movie Groundhog's Day. She declined three invites to go out, including one from Becca, but they were all the same: drinks somewhere then dancing at a club. These were plans she always indulged in because she loved the party scene and toeing the line of being outrageous. She used to fill the night drinking with her friends, flirting with eligible men, and sometimes, if the mood was right, going home with someone.

It wasn't like she could do that now, though, given she wasn't legally considered single anymore.

She wondered how Nate was handling it. They hadn't talked since they'd established the rules to survive their ninety-day stint as being a couple. It was time to give her husband a call. She figured he was probably out since it was a Saturday night, but she planned to leave him a funny voicemail over their oxymoron situation of the century.

"Hey," he answered gruffly.

"Oh, you answered." She sat back in surprise.

"Why did you call if you didn't want me to answer?"

Valid point, but she had prepared a song to leave as a voicemail. It was her one of her ways of coping. If she couldn't have fun, she could annoy others with song—which typically ended up with her being entertained.

"I thought you'd be out." Like she should have been, she thought grimly. "It's midnight in New York. Isn't that the equivalent of time to party?"

"It is when you can fuck someone." Nate sounded like someone had peed in his Cheerios.

She curled up on the couch in her living room. "We agreed anything with clothes on was okay to do with someone else."

He grunted. "I have no desire to make out with someone and leave."

So, Nate wasn't into kissing. Which was a bummer. He had sexy lips. Kissing lips. Lips she definitely wouldn't have minded putting hers on.

"Someone didn't have fun playing spin the bottle when they were in high school," she joked. It was her attempt to lighten the mood. No matter what, Nate was her friend, and he deserved some cheering up.

Finally, he chuckled. "I actually never played. Didn't need to."

"My cocky friend is back." She clapped so he could hear. "And everyone should have to play spin the bottle at some point in their life. We should play when I visit next weekend."

There was a pause, and Samantha was quick to realize what had him speechless: the idea of them kissing and actually remembering it. She had to backtrack. That had not been her intension.

"Ew, we're not playing spin the bottle just the two of us! This isn't about you and me kissing. Gross. You should throw a small party at your apartment. I'll be the hostess with the mostest and suggest the game," she clarified. Even though the image of them kissing didn't seem too bad.

"Fine, but I'm trying not to be angry you think kissing me would be gross."

"I guess we'll find out because we need to capture some pictures of us being a couple."

"The pictures have to include kissing?" Nate asked, as if the idea had never crossed his mind. How lucky for him since she was now thinking about it multiple times a day.

She wouldn't admit it to him, but ever since they'd gotten hitched, she'd spent way too much time daydreaming about Nate and his kissy lips.

"Sure do." Samantha was matter of fact about it. She grabbed a pillow and tucked it behind her head. "We need to prove to the judge we tried."

"Should we make another rule or something?" Nate continued with his questions, sounding unsure about this whole kissing thing.

No need for him to get all grumpy.

It wasn't like they were going to make out, just a kiss here or there. Adding a rule would make it uptight and boring. She couldn't handle any more boring in her life. "No way. We don't get to have sex for three months, the least we can do is enjoy kissing each other instead of making it manufactured. There's no way it would get out of control, you know? And you better watch out, Nate—I'll be the best damn kiss you ever had." It was as if her voice had a mind of its own, flirting with him in a sultry tone.

"Challenge accepted," he responded, flirting right back. His voice was sexy, deep, and seductive. What was worse was how much she liked it. "I promise you, after we kiss, you'll compare every other man to me."

He didn't say goodbye, just hung up. Whether he'd meant to do it or not, she wasn't sure, but the rest of her night, all she thought about was Nate and whether he could live up to his words of being that good of a kisser.

. . .

"YOU'RE PLAYING LIKE shit," Nate's friend Todd passed the ball to him aggressively.

He was playing basketball with his friends, and his game was off, but he hadn't been expecting to get called out over it.

"So? You always play like shit," Nate snarked back, tossing the ball back to him.

Peter, his other friend, stole the ball and scored another point. "You both play like shit."

Todd gave him the middle finger as he sat down on the court.

Nate and some of his friends met up weekly to play. Besides Peter and Todd, Marquis and Devon normally joined too. It was cardio and time to shoot the shit, so Nate hardly missed a game. They played in a vacant court in Hell's Kitchen, which was close to his apartment so there wasn't a good excuse to miss the work out.

Peter slumped down next to him. "This is the only workout I get."

"Outside of chasing after Fiona, same for me." Todd and his wife Lola had a baby girl last year. Whenever he could, he gabbed about it. Nate didn't predict he'd have any of his own kids in his future, but fatherhood looked good on his friend.

"What are you fools doing this weekend?" Nate asked, sitting next to the other two on the court.

"Nothing," Peter answered first. "You flaked on going out last weekend. Let's do something."

Todd stretched his legs out. "Lola and I are visiting my parents in Boston. They haven't seen Fiona in two weeks and are acting like it's been a year so there's no way I can get out of it."

"I want to have some people over on Saturday night," Nate informed them all business-like. It was all he could muster. Ever since this damn marriage happened, it was like he was on autopilot until the annulment.

Todd laughed. "Am I so far removed from the single life that whoring around has changed from bar hopping to small house parties?"

"Fuck you," Nate said half-heartedly so he didn't focus on how he was no longer part of the single scene. "You remember my friend Samantha? She's visiting and I thought a party would be fun."

"Peter, you have to go," Todd urged him while moving his legs in front of him for a better stretch. "I met Samantha before —when I was single, I would like to add—and she was hot. Like, hotter than any of the girls you two idiots manage to hook up with."

Peter lifted an eyebrow. "I was planning to go either way. But why would I want to see her? If she's visiting, I bet she's his friend with benefits."

"Not at all," Todd responded before Nate could. "He always gives this big speech about how they grew up together and it's not like that."

Peter was another person who loved the single life, but he'd claimed many times that he'd settle down and have a family when he met the right woman. Nate had to make sure Peter was aware Samantha wasn't the right woman for him. Technically, even if they weren't telling anyone, she was married, so she wasn't even a viable option.

"It's not like that," Nate lied, turning his gaze to Peter. "But I still don't want you chasing after her."

His friends both had confused looks on their faces but didn't say anything. Conversation went back to Fiona and how she was the fastest crawler alive. It was a relief for Nate. The new topic eased the pit in his stomach. Thinking of Samantha being with someone else made him feel off.

By the time he got home, Samantha was still on his mind.

They had texted here and there but hadn't talked on the phone since she announced they were adding kissing to their to-do list.

He replayed their conversation over and over again. The easy flow of talking to each other had spiraled into something they hadn't done before: flirting.

Since when did he flirt with Samantha?

Apparently, the answer was ever since they got hitched. And what was even more interesting, was that he liked this new version of them.

When they last talked, he'd had to get off the phone with her or he was going to cross a line. The line called initiating phone sex. He was starting to crave her, and he didn't know what to do about it. His work schedule was normally busy, but if he didn't have a hammer in his hand or wasn't telling someone what to do, his mind drifted to Samantha. It was dangerous territory he was stepping in but stopping wasn't an option.

This annulment couldn't come soon enough.

CHAPTER 5

LAGUARDIA AIRPORT WAS bustling, so it was easy for Nate to people watch while he waited for Samantha's flight to land. The tourists were the easiest people to spot. Most clutched tightly on to maps and were looking around like someone was going to mug them at any minute. The locals abruptly pushed past the people slowing them down in pure New York fashion.

"Nate!" Samantha hollered in his direction as she walked toward him. She only had a carry on with her, a pink cotton duffle bag with white and yellow flowers all over it. It was something he loved about her. She was low-key and didn't pack more clothes than the minimal she needed but had some flare with the giant dandelions on her bag.

He grabbed the bag from her and threw it over his shoulder. She yanked his arm and dragged him over to the wall so they weren't in foot traffic.

"Do you plan on spending all weekend in the airport?" he teased while she pulled out her phone to take a selfie. If somebody else were people watching, Samantha would have immediately been tagged as an out of towner because she was taking pictures in the airport.

She looped her arm around his neck and pulled him closer

so they were cheek to cheek. "I'm capturing our marriage, duh. Pretend to be happy like we're trying to work on things."

Click, click, click. She took a handful of pictures before putting her phone away.

"Okay, grumpy pants. Let's head to your apartment."

He mumbled he wasn't grumpy, but she was either ignoring him or didn't hear him between her constant chatter of everything she wanted to do over the weekend.

They got into a cab and headed to Manhattan when she nudged him. "What happened to my fun partner in crime? And if you say lack of sex, I will punch you in the balls."

"Ouch." The taxi driver shuddered when he heard her threat.

She pointed to the driver. "Exactly. I get the past two weeks haven't been your normal MO, but can you pull an Elsa and let it go for the weekend?"

"Did you just reference Disney in the same sentence as my sex life?"

The taxi driver laughed. "Impressive."

When it came to Samantha, nothing surprised him. She was a walking ball of energy and smiles. It was hard to be in a shitty mood around her because her cheerfulness was contagious.

"Sure did. Come on, for my sake, can you not be all moody?" She swept her dark brown hair over her shoulder. "Puh-lease."

He crossed his arms and sternly responded, "Fine, but we're only going to one tourist trap this weekend."

She agreed all too quickly. They arrived at his apartment, and she jetted out of the taxi, hopping up the steps of the building while Nate paid their fare.

"Don't let that one get away," the driver told him with a head tilt to Samantha.

Nate finally laughed, more so at the situation. "Trust me, I couldn't let go of her if I tried."

He went into his building to find his wife. By the elevator, Nate saw Samantha gabbing with one of his neighbors who lived on the same floor as him, Brenda, a woman in her forties who was married with two children. Whatever Samantha was telling her made her laugh.

Samantha caught Nate watching them, so she waved goodbye to the woman and walked over to him.

"If you're making me take the stairs, I get two tourist attractions." Samantha sounded serious as she lifted her nose in the air.

He guided her back to the elevator. "I won't risk it. What were you and Brenda talking about?"

"I was letting her know we were having a party tomorrow. She's bummed she can't make it. Her husband is traveling and she promised the kids a movie marathon."

He shook his head. Not even ten minutes in his building and she was already making friends.

"Smart move telling her about the party so she won't get pissed if we're too loud." Nate pushed the number fifteen button to get to his floor.

Once they were inside, Nate stopped suddenly, not knowing where to put her bag. He had a two-bedroom apartment, but he used his guest room as an office. It was more affordable to set-up something at home than to rent office space. His crew met him at the houses they remodeled, so he never saw reason to spend the money for space in a building for an office.

Now, though, another place to sleep wasn't an option. It wasn't like they hadn't shared a bed before, but in the past, it was always as friends. Would being married be any different?

"What?" Samantha put her hands on her hips and stared at him. "What are you thinking?"

He gave her a crooked grin. "How committed are you to playing house?"

"If you expect me to wear an apron, you're going to be sorely disappointed."

Hmm, Samantha in an apron—only an apron—sounded sexy as hell. He took a deep breath to remove the naughty image of her from his head. He didn't need his dick getting hard, let alone when it came to their sleeping arrangements.

"Are you going to be disappointed if we have to share a bed?"

She laughed, loud and unrestrained. When she got herself together, she said, "Nate, that's what I figured. Your couch is more for show when you need to bring clients here to sign paperwork. No offense, but it isn't the best for sleeping. Whenever I visit, we always pass out on your bed. What would be different this time around?"

What would be different? She had a point. To him, ever since they'd tied the knot, he'd had thoughts about Samantha he'd never had before. That was the difference.

It was up to him not to make a move.

FRIDAY NIGHT IN New York City was exactly what Samantha needed. Nate took her out for dinner, where she took loads of pictures of them to prove they were at least trying to fall in love. It was all pretend, but they would work. The judge would be pleased to see how goofy they were together. In almost every smiling picture, one of them was making a silly face. When she was looking at the pictures on her phone, one stood out to her as her favorite. It was when she took a selfie and Nate jumped in the picture and kissed her cheek. She would frame that one because it was cute and they were both just enjoying the moment.

After dinner, they went for drinks and dancing. It was the quintessential New York night out. By the time they got back to Nate's apartment, it was after two in the morning. They drank as much water as possible, not making another amateur move like Vegas, and fell asleep watching Netflix in his room.

Oh, how Netflix and chill had changed for her.

In the morning, she stretched in bed and noticed someone was missing.

"Nate," she pseudo-yelled as she walked out of his bedroom.

There he was, brushing his teeth, the bathroom door wide open. She was unable to move as she open-mouth appreciated the view. Nate was hot—all her friends constantly mentioned it, and duh, she wasn't blind. Nate without a shirt was even hotter with his natural muscle on display. But Nate wearing only a towel wrapped around his waist was jaw dropping. Were her eyes fooling her, or was Nate packing down there?

Geesh. This whole no sex thing was really messing with her.

"You want to go out for breakfast?" Nate asked when he looked over his shoulder in her direction.

She shook her head, mostly to stop drooling over him. "It's almost lunch time."

"Do you think they stop serving breakfast because of that?"

"No, but I'll need an hour to get ready. Will you still want breakfast then?"

Nate stepped out of the bathroom and walked over to her. He tucked a piece of her hair behind her ear. "My wife is so high maintenance."

She tapped him on the nose. "My husband appreciates it."

"Like how you appreciate me in a towel?" He lifted an eyebrow. "I caught you staring."

Samantha playfully swatted him away. "Trust me, you'll be the one staring later. It's all part of the high maintenance effect."

"Sure, Sammy." He walked to his room without bothering to turn around.

This new flirting between them was fun. It was like they didn't want their skills to get rusty over the next few months of celibacy. Nothing was going to come out of it. It was innocent, really. Either way, she was making sure he was the one to stare tonight.

THEIR PARTY STARTED at eight, which meant no one arrived until nine. Samantha swore it was a New York thing, being fashionably late, but either way, it bought her more time.

It had been a productive day. They'd been able to go to lunch and buy all the food and drinks they needed, which obviously meant lots of champagne. Whether they were happy about their union didn't mean the celebration should suffer. Luck had been on her side because she'd also been able to swing in a nap and had still gotten ready in time. She'd spent an excruciating amount of time making sure Nate would be the one salivating over her. It was hard for her to forget how sexy it had been seeing water dripping down Nate in only a towel. The man oozed hotness. It was like she'd never appreciated how sexy he was until now. Talk about bad timing.

She wore a black lace dress that hugged her tightly, showing off all her curves. The dress was one of her favorites because it came mid-thigh and was long sleeved but had an open back. She liked to call this look librarian in the front, party in the back.

On a normal day, Samantha's dark hair fell straight down below her shoulders. Tonight, however, she'd been aiming for a glamorous style to match her sexy dress. She set her hair in curlers while she applied smokey eye makeup and red lipstick. Okay, she'd had to multi-task and watch a YouTube video on how to do the makeup, but it had worked.

After she released the curlers, she smiled. She was a sex-vixen. Nate was definitely going to break his neck looking at her. It made her smile, the idea of him checking her out.

Soft music played in the background, and she heard the pop of a champagne bottle. The whole theme for the evening was Bubbly and Babes. She made sure she was in charge of the e-vite so everyone dressed up and was prepared to party. If she would have left it to Nate, he would have just sent a text message telling people about the night.

The bedroom door pushed open, and Nate hollered, "Hurry up and get out here. I'm sick of explaining to everyone how I didn't design the stupid invitation."

With that, he went back to the party, not once turning around to glance at her. Some husband he was turning out to be.

Ready to make her grand entrance, she left the bedroom and waltzed into the living room, where about twenty guests were mingling around. People were laughing, eating snacks, and sharing stories about their week. It was the perfect party.

Edison and Tim she had known for years from visiting Nate in the past, so she made her way over to them to say hello. They had both worked for him, so there were bound to be shared stories of how Nate was such a strict boss. It made her smile. She turned to look for him, but he was nowhere to be seen. He had a small patio, so he was probably out there.

"Samantha," Edison lifted her into a big embrace, "you get more and more beautiful every time I see you."

"I'm like fine wine," she said cheekily.

Tim gave her a hug as well. "Looking good, Sammy."

"I need to come to the city more often if I'm going to get compliments like this," she said sweetly.

Edison shook his head. "After all these years, Nate still isn't giving in?"

This was news. Giving in to what?

While she really wanted a glass of champagne, she put it off to badger Edison for more detail. "Care to share more?" She gave him her poutiest smile to make him cave.

Tim let out a deep chuckle. "Please. You and the boss have been dancing around each other ever since we met you."

"Exactly," Edison chimed in. "When are you two going to sleep together already?"

"And if it actually isn't happening with Nate, go to dinner with me." Tim put his hands together like he was pleading with her.

"Absolutely not." Nate had found the perfect opportunity to join their conversation. His hand rested on the bare skin of her lower back, giving her an electric chill. Nate touching her was sensory overload. Topping it off was how much she enjoyed it. "Leave her alone."

"Told you," Edison mumbled as he grabbed Tim's elbow and shuffled them away.

Standing alone in a corner of a party was not how she imagined her Saturday night.

"You owe me a drink since you chased off the two friends I have here." She moved so they were face to face.

The glare he had shot his friends didn't soften when he looked at her. "Tim was trying to sleep with you," he clipped.

"And if you didn't shut him down on that subject, I would have. I wouldn't sleep with one of your friends."

His hand reached out, and his fingertips gently traveled up her arm. "What is this dress?"

There went more chills. His touch was addictive.

"Trina Turk," she blankly named the designer as she struggled with how much she loved his hands on her.

She looked up at him, and he gave her a sinister smile—one she has never said no to in the past because it meant they were going to have fun or cause trouble, possibly both. Now, though, it was promising trouble.

"How angry would you be if I ended the party?"

"Depends," she sauntered back. "Are you going to give me another option for entertainment?"

"Party's over!" he yelled, never taking his eyes off her. All the noise stopped, and he shouted out again, "Party's over. I know it's only ten, but feel free to take the champagne with you."

"I paid for that," she protested.

His eyes darkened. "I promise I'll make up for it."

Oh boy, how she was loving every second of Nate changing the dynamic. Something was simmering and with the look Nate gave her, it was about to explode between them. Samantha was burning up waiting for everyone to leave. Why did it feel like it was taking forever? She had no idea what to expect, but she wanted whatever Nate was going to give her.

One by one, all the guests took their time saying their goodbyes and leaving with bottles of her champagne. It didn't matter. Samantha was seconds away from pushing them out the door. It was like every single person wanted to hug them before they left.

Nate and Samantha stared at each other the entire time, regardless of the people who stopped to talk to them. Their guests must have sensed the buzzing chemistry coursing through them, because in another ten minutes, everyone was gone.

Finally, it was just Samantha and Nate.

CHAPTER 6

THE TENSION WAS brewing between them and the air was crackling. After Nate unceremoniously ended the party and people waltzed off with her booze, it was time for one of them to man up. They needed to talk about this undercurrent between them. Instead of either of them taking action, they just stared at each other, circling around the chemistry about to ignite.

Samantha took the silence as a retreat. Nate was backtracking now that they were alone. Perhaps he had a moment of sanity and realized this magnetic pull was something better left ignored. She took a step away from him and turned around. She had to, or his hypnotic eyes were going to make her say screw it and kiss the ever-loving shit out of him.

She needed a safe haven—which was the kitchen. Without anything better to do, she started cleaning up. Not her favorite thing in the world, but it would pass the time while she overanalyzed what had just happened. She knew her way around Nate's kitchen since she had been the one who'd helped him organize everything when he'd moved in, so she had no trouble bagging up all the trash.

The silence was eerily surrounding her, almost like a taunt

to go check on the man in the other room, but she refused to see what he was doing. She stood at the sink, cleaning the plates and setting them on the other side of the sink. Who didn't have a damn dishwasher in the millennium was beyond her, but she planned to dry the plates once she was done. Having a step-by-step process was calming her down.

Instead of debating whether she should be stripping off Nate's clothes and demanding he do the same to her, she was scraping spinach dip off his plates. And with each plate, came more anger on her end.

Why would he end the party and then have the balls to just ignore her?

Even if he didn't want more to happen, didn't she deserve an explanation?

She was his wife.

It was the least he could do.

As her irritation grew, she began wreaking havoc on the plates. Suds and water flew everywhere as she aggressively cleaned with annoyance. This was like Cinderella gone wild— all she was missing was the blonde hair and singing mice friends.

This was his kitchen. These were his plates. She stomped her foot. While this was a far cry from barefoot and pregnant, she wasn't going to clean his kitchen while he did whatever he wanted in the living room.

Besides, he ended the party. He should have to be the one to clean. Not her.

THE SOUND OF plates crashing into the sink made Nate snicker. Glancing at his watch, he confirmed it had taken Sammy a total of fifteen minutes in the kitchen before she lost her shit. He was surprised it had taken her that long. She was never one to back down or ignore the elephant in the room.

"If you think I'm just going to clean up from the party *you* ended and go to bed," she stomped into the living room, one hand on her hip, the other pointing a finger at him, "you have seriously lost your mind. I mean, you stopped a party then—"

Both her hands dropped when she saw him.

Nate was sitting on the floor, his legs sprawled out in front of him, his hand resting behind him, a smirk on his face.

She started to giggle, and the sweet sound reassured his decision.

Then that giggle turned into full on chuckling.

Okay, maybe this wasn't reassuring.

"Do you know," she said, wiping away tears from her laughter, soap stuck in her hair, "I was about to come out here and go full on crazy wife? I was cleaning plates, pissed you ended the party and then did nothing."

Nate lifted the side of his mouth while she spoke. She was animated, always using her hands to talk, her eyes lighting up with her words.

"I'm serious. Every time I picked something up or wiped something down, I was ready to smack you."

Pushing off his hands so he was sitting up, he pointed at the empty champagne bottle in front of him. "You promised you'd play spin the bottle with me. You left, and I've been sitting here waiting for you."

Purposely, he left out the whole self-reflection of how kissing her might change everything. How he was scared out of his mind that he might not be able to stop wanting more of her once he knew how she tasted. Ever since they got married, he couldn't help but think maybe they should actually try the whole husband and wife thing a try and see where things go. His mind was clearly playing tricks on him, so he decided to ignore all of it—even if it was starting to make more sense to him.

His only goal at the moment was to kiss her. Fuck the rest.

Samantha sat down across from him on the floor.

"You are right. I did promise to play."

Her hands were shaky as she brushed her curls over her shoulder. He watched her sit up straight and tuck away her nerves about playing the childhood game. For a second, he wondered if she also thought it was ridiculous they were using the excuse of a game to initiate their first kiss. As if spin the bottle could take the fallout if anything negative happened between them.

She moved the champagne bottle so it was symmetrical between them. "Here are the rules."

He rolled his eyes. "I should have known."

"Says someone who's never played before."

"You've never played football, but you know the rules of the game," he countered.

She teasingly glared at him. "Shush. I'm in charge here since I've played before. We spin the bottle and kiss who it lands on."

"Thanks for clearing that up," he said sarcastically. "Who spins first?"

"Me, because I'm the youngest."

"By a few months," he protested. He wasn't sure if it was nerves of knowing he was about to kiss her or if he just wanted to be the one who spun the bottle. "This is my house."

She tipped her head to the side. "This is my bottle of champagne."

"Fine."

He stopped arguing. His need to kiss her was far more important. It was finally going to happen. Every moment since they'd gotten hitched had been leading to this.

Samantha spun the bottle. It finally stopped and pointed at the chair.

He couldn't handle it anymore. The desire—no, more like the need—to have her mouth on his was unbearable. It was as if his life depended on knowing how soft her lips were. He had to confirm if she tasted as sweet as he suspected. He had to hear if she moaned when he slipped his tongue into her mouth. The anticipation was too much.

"Fuck this," he said before smacking the bottle from between them. He heard it hit the wall but didn't bother to look. Without a second thought, they both moved to their knees, bodies flushed against each other.

His hands gripped the back of her hair, pulling her head back. He growled out, "Fuck anymore waiting."

HIS MOUTH CRUSHED against hers, sending waves of desire pulsing through her. His lips were possessive and desperate as he demanded everything from her, and Samantha gave him everything he asked for. She wiggled against him, unable to control her body from rubbing against his, desperate for the friction. Samantha was needy for him and wanted more.

He bit her lower lip, and she moaned as his tongue slipped into her mouth. It was an intense moment as he took his time devouring her mouth, tasting her with every rub of his tongue. Nate was in complete control as he angled her head so he could deepen the kiss, his hands never letting go of the back of her neck as he gently tugged her hair.

Holy hell, this kiss was the best of her life. Sensations coursed through her while her body trembled with desire.

A soft whimper squeaked out of her as his hands dropped from her neck. Her needy noise must have sparked something in him because he sat back on the floor and pulled her on top of him so she was in his lap. The entire time, his lips never left hers. They were drunk off the kiss alone.

It was like they were made for each other. They fit perfectly together.

She grinded against him and groaned again. This time, she

felt his hard cock sliding against her through his jeans. Now, she no longer had to question whether he was packing or not. He was thick and long even in his pants. Holy hell, she needed to see him naked.

His hands gripped her hips as she swayed over top of him as if they were having sex. He controlled the speed of her movement, and she loved his aggressive grasp. His hands were sure to leave a mark, and that turned her on even more. The only thing stopping them from fucking were the clothes they were still wearing. The moment was sexy and mind consuming. She leaned back, just for a second, to take her shirt off, but Nate stopped her.

"Fuck," he muttered. His hands dropped to the floor. "What the fuck are we doing?"

With those words, all the magic was sucked out of the room.

CHAPTER 7

"**I THOUGHT WE** were kissing," Samantha answered defiantly, her arms crossed. It was pitiful, but her only defense mechanism at the moment was to act as though what just happened meant nothing.

Which was a complete lie.

"Don't look at me like that," Nate barked as he scrambled to get away from her. He moved so quick, he was already standing by the window on the other side of the room by the time her butt hit the ground.

It was a good assumption they were done playing spin the bottle.

"How am I looking at you?" she snapped back.

He ran his hands through his hair, refusing to make eye contact or respond to her question. Staring out the window was apparently far more intriguing than the fact that they were just mauling each other with sex on the horizon.

Samantha moved over to him and poked his shoulder in anger. "Now isn't the time to admire the city. You ended a party where people, including me, were having fun. Then you decide to kiss the hell out of me like I was all you wanted. And now you pull back and tell me not to look at you *like that*. Do tell, how am I looking at you?"

Nate, being four inches taller, stared down at her. "Like you want something that'll ruin everything."

"Didn't you kiss me?"

"We were playing the game."

This made her laugh—and not the good kind. It was almost manic, like she couldn't believe this was actually happening. What a lame excuse, blaming their chemistry on a game. "Are you serious?"

"As serious as our signed contract," he said, a touch of bitterness in his tone.

She flipped her hair over her shoulder before putting her hands on her hips. "Don't you dare act like this is my fault. Our sham of a marriage wasn't something I forced on you. It wasn't like I woke up in a committed relationship and celebrated the news. We're in the same boat here."

He huffed. "I know it's not your fault we're married."

"Wow, you sound so sincere." Her voice oozed sarcasm.

"It isn't either of our faults," he conceded. "But it was stupid for us to kiss for no reason. We need to follow the rules. I'm going to hold up my end of the bullshit bargain."

If kissing her senseless was part of holding up his end of the bargain, she wasn't sure she'd survive anymore of their marriage. Her lips were bruised at the way he'd devoured her. Her pulse was still racing over the excitement of feeling his hands on her.

Now, with his mightier than thou attitude, she wanted to take a shower. Wash away his touch.

"Our marriage is a bargain," she repeated his words. "I've never felt so cheap."

He groaned, looking up at the ceiling for a second. "You know that's not what a meant. You aren't a bargain, but our marriage is a fucking joke. Like you pointed out, neither of us want this. We promised this wouldn't change anything, and we need to remember that."

Oh, she was going to remember this exact moment forever.

When they'd kissed, all she could think, outside of get this man naked, was how good it was between them. It was a shame it had taken them so long to cross the hooking up line. Not anymore. She wished she could take it all back.

"Let's just stick to the rules and we only kiss when we're doing it for a picture." He sounded like a teacher reprimanding a student.

"Got it," she clipped back. Her hands hadn't moved from her hips because she was afraid they would be shaking with anger.

"No sex is one of those rules." His eyes narrowed at her.

She glared at him. "I'm sorry. Did I sleep with someone since Vegas and somehow forgot about it?"

"Don't be coy."

"Don't tell me what to do."

"We can't fuck this up. We're married and have rules."

"Rules I didn't break!" she yelled. It was uncharacteristic of her, but Nate had made her lose her cool.

"I never should have..." He paused, almost as if he didn't want to finish his sentence.

Samantha stomped her foot in frustration. "If you have something to say to me, say it."

"I'll sleep on the couch tonight."

Not bothering with a response, she stormed off to his bedroom and slammed the door. She threw on her pajamas and laid in bed, rustling around trying to fall asleep. It was bad enough his kiss had left her all hot and bothered, but then it had turned into a fight. Their first fight as a married couple—and they didn't even get to have make-up sex.

Marriage was the worst.

. . .

THE NEXT MORNING came, and Nate dreaded seeing her again. It was a whole different morning after. When Samantha marched into the living room, she looked so good, she took his breath away. She had always been a head turner, but since their kiss, he'd been seeing her in a new light. A very attractive new light. He was afraid to touch her because he was sure to get burned.

Last night, he hadn't been able to sleep at all. Not only had he replayed their kiss in his head all night, which had been hot as fuck even if it was a stupid move he'd also wondered what would happen next between them. It also didn't help that his couch wasn't winning any awards for being comfortable. That thing was stiff as a board.

He sat up, hiding his groan about having a sore back, and listened to Samantha sing.

Sing.

She was singing.

Just like his couch, she wasn't going to win any awards for her voice. Her pitch sounded like a cat shrieking.

Once she came back into the living room, she gave him a blank stare. "I'm going to the airport. I'll try not to fuck anybody on the flight. You know, since you suggested I'm not good at following rules."

Despite her awful voice, he almost wished she'd kept singing. It was better than having his words thrown back in his face.

Well...almost. She really couldn't carry a tune.

Her attitude and snarky comments were begging him for a fight. Couldn't she do the normal thing and pretend last night didn't happen? That was his game plan.

"Thanks for the reassurance," he said dryly.

Something soft whacked him in the head. Once she was out the door, he realized she'd thrown a pillow at him. The silence in the room, which he always loved, felt empty.

The silence that had been there ever since the judge ruled they had to try in their marriage for ninety days. That was when Nate's world had shifted. For as long as he could remember, any time he'd had a sexual thought about Samantha, he'd filed it away in an imaginary box he'd never planned to open. It was Samantha.

His friend since childhood.

The female version of himself.

Then he had to fuck it all up and kiss her.

Now, he knew how she tasted, how she moaned, how she felt. That imaginary box was wide open, and all the sexual thoughts were floating around him.

Nate was grappling with the idea of Samantha being more than a friend. Before the party, when he'd walked into his bedroom and she had been getting ready, his heart had stopped. She'd looked like every sexual fantasy come to life.

Those emotions weren't real. He had to remind himself that every time he wished she was more than just a friend.

As he paced around his apartment, he assured himself this need to fuck Samantha was fleeting. Samantha was the forbidden fruit. She always had been. A court order stating they couldn't sleep together was the reason he was attracted to her. He wanted what he couldn't have.

It explained everything.

He smiled when he grabbed an icepack out of the freezer for his back. This magnetic pull he had to Samantha was because he couldn't have sex and, most notable, wasn't supposed to touch her. If he did, it was goodbye to an easy annulment.

The only thing he had to do was stop obsessing over the lack of sex in his life. He had to ignore his curiosity of what it would be like to fuck his wife. He had to stop fantasizing over her. His hard-on wasn't worth losing a friendship over. Look at the damage he'd already caused.

She deserved an apology, and he needed his friend back.

CHAPTER 8

AFTER LETTING ONE day pass, time was ticking for Nate to stop messing around and apologize to Samantha. After she'd left, he'd switched heat and ice every twenty minutes on his back, leaving him with plenty of time to sulk about how much of an ass he had been. He was close to labeling himself a five-stage clinger the way he obsessed over her. It was bad.

"Boss, the recessed kitchen vents are mounted," one of his contractors, Donny, shouted to him from the kitchen. "You were right, the ceiling mount looks sharp and modernizes the kitchen."

He joined him in the kitchen, along with six others working on the remodel of the latest house he planned to flip. Everyone had worked their asses off. He imagined the house would be done within the next month.

Grabbing the remote control from the marble countertop, he made sure the vents were noiseless as they opened in the ceiling above the stovetop. He had been busy striping the paint off the walls in the living room, so it was the first time he'd checked the kitchen. The electrical outlets were installed, the kitchen sink was wall-mounted, and the cabinets were painted.

"Everyone can go home," Nate announced, gliding his hand

over the newly installed countertops. "Great job today. If we keep up this pace, we can take Friday off."

His team appreciated this. They cheerfully saluted him as they all left. Standing alone in the house, he pulled out his phone and called Samantha. The longer he delayed the well-deserved apology, the more trouble he was going to be in.

"Hey," she answered, her voice back to being upbeat. Damn, he loved that about her. Her positive attitude was always there, even if he didn't deserve it.

"On a scale of one to ten, how much trouble am I in?" Nate decided to get it together and treat her like a friend—what he should've been doing the whole time.

Her faint giggle made him smile. When it came to wives, he'd definitely hit a gold mine. There was an authentic air about her, something open and honest and transparent, that was sexy as hell. She'd gotten the short end of the stick since she was stuck with him.

"That depends. Are we only considering your asshole move on how you treated me Saturday or that it took you this long to actually call me?" She put all the cards on the table.

"Oh, wait," she continued, "or is this about how you canceled the party and gave away all my champagne?"

Before he could interject, she continued, "Or is this about the elephant in the room? Do you want me to forgive you for that mediocre kiss?"

Wait one fucking second. A mediocre kiss?

"Bullshit on the kiss," he immediately contradicted her, not touching on anything else she'd pointed out.

"Then, please, do tell what this apology is for." Her words may have been tough, but he swore he could hear the smile in her tone.

Samantha was someone who was all about forgive and forget. She claimed holding a grudge took up too much of her time. She had always been like that, never one to hang something over someone's head. Even when they were kids, she'd been a badass like that.

"I'm sorry I was an ass."

"About what?" She was relentless for making him grovel.

"You aren't going to make this easy?" Not that he deserved it, but he'd been hoping her history of no drama would come into play.

"No way. I want to hear what you have to say for all the bullshit."

He sat on one of the step ladders in the kitchen.

"Fair. First, I'm sorry I was a dick Saturday. Both for the things I said about our whole situation and for taking this long to call you and apologize. I never should have let you leave without telling you how much you mean to me."

She didn't respond, probably because it was so glaringly obvious.

"You were excited to throw the party, and I shouldn't have ended it the way I did. But I'd like to point out, I didn't give away all the champagne. Which comes to my next point."

"And what point is that?"

"Our kiss was not mediocre, and you damn well know it."

"Debatable," she returned all too quickly for his liking.

Fuck, his ego was taking a hit right now.

"I'm not going to argue. You and I both know the truth about that kiss. I'm sorry I was an idiot and didn't treat you like a friend. Sammy, you've always been one of my closest friends. I promise not to act like an asshole again." He was teetering on pleading for her forgiveness.

"Okay." She paused, as if she needed to think things over. "I forgive you. But only because you sound hopeless right now. Pathetic, really."

They both laughed, and he was relieved. "Either way, you owe me."

"Wait, wait, wait. You mess up and this ends in me owing you? This isn't how apologies work, my friend."

My friend.

Two words he'd never anticipated would make his skin crawl.

What the hell was happening to him?

"You're on east coast time, but here in my world, it's midday, so chaos is around the corner. Can we chat later? I can't wait to hear how I owe you," she informed him as he heard the beeping and pinging from her computer over the phone.

They only talked for another minute before saying goodbye. Which was fine with him. He never looked forward to long talks on the phone.

It was fine, really.

AFTER A RUN in Central Park and revising plans to finalize a sale for a house he'd finished remodeling last month, he was exhausted. Nate had never been cut out for a corporate job, having a nine to five in an office. Working with his hands and managing the daily changes he made to a house invigorated him.

Today, he was testing himself. After reconstructing a light fixture in his own house then working out, paperwork was the last thing he wanted to do. If it was for a hefty paycheck on selling a house, though, he would never procrastinate. Not normally. Money made the world go round—and it was how he paid his employees.

But there had been a change in his life.

For months, something had been off. When he considered expanding his business from the east coast to back home in San Francisco, he hadn't wasted a second coming up with a business plan on how to make it work. The goal was to transition from remodeling houses to restoring older, historic homes. With his latest sale, he was close to hitting his goal for making Haddic Historic Restorations a reality.

His phone buzzed with a text. He couldn't stop the smile when he saw it was from Samantha.

I can't believe you managed to annoy me so much, I had to get wine after work.

His smile vanished. How in the hell could she be upset with him again? He didn't wait to respond.

You can't be that mad if you're drinking wine. You love wine.

Okay, he was being a little flirty, but it seemed to make them both happy.

You're right. But all day I wondered how I owed you something. You better fess up.

He grinned while he texted. *You owe me because I had to sleep on that shit couch.*

Nate sent the message before he could double guess it. The bubbles popped up, acknowledging she was responding, then disappeared. They appeared again, then they were gone. He left his phone on the coffee table and went into the kitchen to get a beer. When he got back to the couch, he had a message from her.

I'd love to hear how this is my fault.

A smile came across his face. Talking to her was the best way to end his day.

YIKES. HE WAS calling. Since when did Samantha get butterflies from Nate calling? As soon as he'd kissed her.

Ugh.

She took a deep breath to get herself in check, then she answered.

"Hello," she said, doing her best to control the excitement in her voice. "Before I hear any silly excuses about me owing you anything, you slept on the couch because you were an asshole."

His deep chuckle gave her goosebumps. She did have the AC and a fan on in her bedroom, so she blamed the temperature —anything to be the culprit for her tingly reaction, really— anything but her husband.

"Fine, but if we ever fight again, we need to make up before I sleep on the couch. My back still hurts because I care more about the aesthetics of my living room than comfort."

She shook her head, even though he couldn't see her. "I don't feel bad for you at all. You should get an actual office so you don't need clients to come to your apartment and see your décor."

"It's more affordable this way. Renting space for an office is ridiculous when it isn't required. Anyway, you should feel bad for me, I still haven't technically played spin the bottle. Only one of us went."

Why was he bringing this up? They needed to reestablish some rules. Kissing and flirting were starting to become way too much for her, despite how much she craved it.

"It's probably better that way," she replied after taking a sip of wine. "Married couples don't play spin the bottle."

"You don't think so?" his sexy voice questioned her.

"Oh, speaking of marriage," Samantha said, not at all casually. "Let's talk about that rule with kissing. Did we decide on adding no more kissing unless it's for a picture to our rules?"

He didn't respond, which was either really good or really bad. To keep control, as flimsy as she had it, she kept talking.

"I know you brought it up when you were freaking out, but maybe you're right. Kissing is blurring the lines. We have rules, and, okay, at first kissing was acceptable, but now that we did it, it's like, why do it again?"

"Uh huh." He sounded amused by her rambling.

Now that the word vomit had been initiated, she couldn't stop herself from blabbing.

"We just pretend like we never kissed. So, no more talking about it since it never happened."

Nate coughed like something was stuck in his throat. "Before we pull a *Fight Club* on the kiss, can I ask a question?"

"Ugh, fine." She would answer whatever stupid question he had, then it was game over for their kissing experiment.

"Are you adding the no kissing unless it's for a picture rule because you're afraid of how much you enjoy kissing your husband?"

This conversation was heading down the wrong path again. If he kept talking to her like that, she was going to demand phone sex. His voice was way too sultry, way too sexy, and just way too Nate. She had to nip this in the bud.

Back to their rules and keeping boundaries.

"Please, kissing you was the worst." She sat up straight, as if her posture would make her believe her words. "Gross. You're like a brother to me."

"Right, gross." His response wasn't too convincing. "Well, I'll be visiting next week. Let's make a promise not to get into another fight."

They made the promise and quickly got off the phone, as if they both knew the conversation was toeing their delicate line of friendship. Marriage was a hell of a lot more complicated than people ever talked about.

IT WAS AFTER ten at night, but Nate was too wired to sleep. After talking with Samantha, there was immediate relief since they weren't fighting anymore, but now he was noticing things about her, like how sexy her voice was. She could be a sex phone operator if she needed to switch careers. He shut his eyes as he relaxed on his bed and imagined kissing away her stupid idea of him being like a brother to her.

There was something else in the air between them, and they both knew it.

All he could think about was the black lace dress she wore the night he'd lost his damn control and kissed her.

She was the sexiest woman he'd ever laid his eyes on.

He wasn't blind, he had always known Samantha was a walking wet dream, but keeping her in the friend-zone had saved him from treating her like any of the other women he met. There was no way he could fuck Samantha and walk away.

It wasn't just because their families were friends.

He had the nagging thought she was the one woman he wouldn't be able to get enough of. Samantha would be a game changer.

He bit his lower lip while the image of Samantha clouded his thoughts. Her creamy skin he now had first-hand knowledge was soft to touch. His hand slipped into his gym shorts and slowly gripped his stiff cock. He wasn't a saint. Thinking of Samantha made him so hard it hurt. He needed a release.

This time around, since she was his wife, even if they weren't crossing the intimacy line with each other in a physical sense, he was finally going to give in to thinking about her while he touched himself. He stroked his hard shaft, dreaming it was Samantha's hands on him.

The mere thought of fucking Samantha had him on fire. His orgasm pumped through him like a wildfire. He was out of breath and couldn't believe one of the best orgasms he'd had in a long time was by his hand with thoughts of Samantha.

This marriage was getting out of control.

WHILE AT WORK the next day, Samantha effortlessly created a new marketing campaign to run on Twitter. Social media was a valuable tool, and the company she worked for gained followers every day for their new credit card release. She emailed the new marketing material to the chief officers of the organization since they had to sign-off on everything before she could distribute.

Becca knocked on her office door, peeking her head in. "Free for a few?"

Samantha was. She motioned for her friend to come in. "I just sent some promotion ideas to leadership since they take a week or so for approval. I hope I can run it at end of month. It looks sharp. I only made a few tweaks from our team meeting last week."

"Nice." Becca nodded while flopping down in the chair across from Samantha's desk. "I'm bugging you to see what your plans are for this weekend."

She shrugged, unsure if she had anything concrete. Nate was visiting for a week, but that didn't mean she was going to see him over the weekend. "Undecided at the moment. Why, what do you have going on?"

"I have another date with Teddy on Saturday. He has a younger brother, Matty, who's equally as hot." She wagged her eyebrows.

"Teddy and Matty? I'm trying not to be judgy on their names right now," Samantha chuckled.

Becca giggled while lightly tapping her foot on the edge of the desk. "You're failing at that effort. Anyway, it's going to be fun."

"Where are you guys going?" she asked.

Her brown eyes were filled with excitement. "Taking a drive to Redwood Park. Matty wants to go with us."

"I hope Matty likes being a third wheel. You should tell him to bring a book or something. Does he fish?"

"Geez, do I need to spell it out for you?" Becca sounded agitated.

Her phone vibrated with a text from Nate. This would be their first time talking without any more discussion of the infamous kiss. She hoped to hell she wasn't blushing since she was remembering how turned on she'd gotten just from speaking to him on the phone.

Flying in Sunday. Want to grab dinner?

Dinner would be fun, and the odds of her demanding more kisses from him were minimal. She was optimistic like that. Quickly, she responded back, so she wasn't rude to her friend.

Sounds perfect. Let's meet at Tony's around 7:30.

Becca knocked on the desk to get her attention. "Sammy, hello? I'm asking you to come with us. You'll love Matty."

This was something she would normally be down for. But it wasn't like she could go on a date with someone who wasn't her husband.

"I can't," she answered without much gusto.

Becca leaned back, surprised. "Why? Just last month you were saying how you were ready to have a new friend with benefits. Matty could be it for you."

Had she said that? Last month felt like a lifetime ago. Last month, she'd been casually seeing men and having fun without consequences. Now, she had a damn husband.

A husband she was struggling to keep in the friend-zone.

"I'm kind of seeing someone."

An awkward truth at its finest.

Another surprised look on Becca's face as her eyes widened. "Is it serious?"

Ha, what a loaded question.

"Um, TBD?" was all she could muster.

Becca stood up to leave. "Okay. Well, if anything changes, you have an option for a double date on Saturday."

Her friend went back to work, and Samantha let out a deep breath. She hadn't had to explain her marital status to anyone, and she was happy for it. The whole thing was so convoluted and full of emotions she didn't know how to handle. There was no way she'd be successful at explaining it.

No matter what, she and Nate were more than casually seeing each other. She was freaking married without any of the sexual benefits. And after their fight last weekend, she had the feeling her husband wouldn't like her on a date with someone else.

CHAPTER 9

AFTER NATE CHECKED into the Hilton at Fisherman's Wharf, he took the time to unpack for his week stay. He did this whenever he traveled, even if it was only for a night. Living out of a suitcase had a melancholy sense to it Nate always tried to avoid.

He had a few hours until he was meeting Samantha for dinner, so he showered to not smell like the airport. The shower was like a reset button. Throwing on jeans and a green t-shirt, he got into his rental car and drove to visit his parents'.

"I'm home," he yelled into the house as he walked in. His mom and stepdad lived outside San Francisco in the house he'd grown up in. He'd been telling them to downsize for years, but his mom wasn't ready.

His mom, Natalie, rushed into the living room to meet him with a giant hug. "I can't believe I get to see you a month after our Vegas vacation! It's normally not so frequent."

She was giddy with excitement over the notion. For a second, he felt like an ass for not visiting more, but work took up more time than he got credit for. He wasn't always in playboy mode, despite what people assumed.

"By the end of the week, you'll be begging me to go back to

New York," he joked as he moved over to his stepdad, Mark, for a hug.

"I doubt that," Mark told him with a smile. "Your mom has told anyone who's been willing to listen about how you were visiting. From the cashier at Bi-Rite Market to our neighbors. Every single one."

They all got comfortable in the living room, Nate stretching on the couch. After the six-hour flight, his long legs felt cramped.

Natalie waved Mark's comments off with a flick of her wrist. "My only son comes for a random visit, I can tell anyone I want. I love having you here, but this is a surprise. Is something going on? Are you all right?"

For a moment, he wondered how it would go if he said, *I got so drunk in Vegas I blackout married your best friend's daughter, and now we have to try to make said marriage work because it was court ordered. In reality, we're just taking pictures pretending we're trying. Oh, and I have constant blue balls because I can't fuck anyone.* He imagined not well, and it wasn't because of the whole blue balls thing. Fake or not, if he was in a relationship, his mom would never let him hear the end of it because of how happy she'd be over the news. Once she discovered it was all pretend with one her closest friends' daughters, she'd be pissed.

She'd probably try to ground him or something, even though it was a futile effort at his age.

"I'm thinking," he paused, not wanting to get his mom's hopes up about him moving back to the west coast, "about expanding the business to focus on historic home restoration. I want to see what the appetite is like out here."

Her smile overtook her face as she grabbed Mark's arm. "So, you'd be in the area more?"

Mark affectionately patted her hand. "How about we don't worry about that until something is set in stone?"

Nate nodded. "Exactly. I'll let you know if or when you can get excited over it."

Her smile turned into the mom look—the one that made him cringe even though she hadn't said a word.

"What?" Nate asked, nervous about her glare.

"Why are you staying in a hotel and not with us? It's bad enough I don't get to see you often, and now you won't sleep here? Why?"

Mark shot him an empathetic look because he must have understood why a hotel was a better option, but it didn't stop the scowl his mom gave him.

"And if you say it's because of your roguish ways, I'll be angry." His mom wasn't messing around. He lifted the corner of his mouth in a grin.

"Roguish ways? Who even says that?" Nate questioned her, his legs still resting out. He swore, the moment he stopped needing to stretch out, he'd be back on the plane for his flight home.

Mark silently shook his head, holding back laughter.

"They say it all the time on *Bridgerton*, but that's not the point."

"The show based in the eighteen-hundreds?" Nate was teasing his mom, but also hoping it would distract her enough to let go of his normal player ways.

"It's a wonderful show, just like it's a wonderful book series." Natalie didn't sound too convincing, but that was probably because she knew she was being veered off course. Her mom sixth sense was strong.

Nate glanced at his watch. It was only five, but he was ready to go. A conversation about his roguish ways was better left unsaid. It wasn't like he wasn't here all week and couldn't see them later.

"I'll have to look into the books." He got up from the couch. "I have a lot of work this week and I'm less distracted at a hotel.

Please don't take it personal, mom. I promise to see you every day, even if it's only for fifteen minutes."

Her face lit up, and she clapped with excitement. "I'm keeping my fingers crossed work will bring you back here to California."

Not one to make empty promises, Nate got up and walked over to his parents. His kissed his mom on the cheek and gave Mark a hug.

"I'm going to dinner with a friend," he told them. "I'll stop by for lunch tomorrow. Does that work?"

They both nodded in agreement, so Nate gave another round of hugs and headed out the door. Something his mother had said kept playing on repeat when he got in his car. Her hope work would keep him local wasn't too far off, but he was starting to believe his career wasn't only work he was coming home for.

A DINNER DATE with Nate was nothing new. They always grabbed food together, but lately, Samantha had noticed a slight shift when it came to him. Obviously, she ignored any idea of sleeping with Nate. However, she didn't want to wear her casual outfit of yoga pants and the oversized Jack Johnson t-shirt. Even if they weren't having sex, she still had the urge to make him want her. It was such a game, but she was willing to play.

It was easy to reason with herself this was normal.

Like, when all was said and annulled, she and Nate would laugh and laugh about how marriage made them horny for each other. It would be a big joke they would find endlessly funny. It would eventually be hysterical how they made out like teenagers in New York. She was sure of it because nothing else would actually transpire between them. It was just more fun for them to flirt and use sexy voices on the phone.

One-hundred-precent the only reason.

Nothing more.

She had an hour before she had to leave to meet him for

dinner, but she wanted to start getting ready. To shower, shave, blow out her hair, apply makeup, and get dressed would take all the time she had left.

Don't judge about shaving. It wasn't because of Nate.

At all.

It was part of her routine.

Mostly.

After her shower, she threw on a clean pair of yoga pants and a baggy t-shirt to get ready. She groaned in frustration as she stared into her closest for an outfit that appeared effortless but screamed sexy. A knock on her door interrupted her search for the perfect get-up.

It was probably Becca. The woman was on the hunt to figure out who had Samantha's attention enough that she'd blow off a random double date. She was pretty persistent.

She hurried off and opened her front door, her mouth dropping when she saw Nate standing there, leaning against her doorframe. He was mouthwatering. She wasn't sure how she'd managed to not crawl all over him in the years they'd been friends.

"Why are you out of breath?" he asked, stepping around her to walk inside her apartment.

She followed after him as he sat on the couch getting comfortable. He looked good in her apartment, like he was meant to be there. Ugh, Nate being sexy on her couch was not needed.

"I'm not out of breath." And she wasn't. She might have been panting, though, which was equally as embarrassing. "And I always love to see you, but weren't we supposed to meet at seven-thirty?"

She stayed standing, hoping a light bulb would go off and remind him he was early. Perhaps he would leave so she could get ready. Rude since it wasn't like he had his own house to go to, but she still had makeup and hair to do.

"I just left my parents and wasn't in the mood to go back to the hotel," he said without a worry in the world. Totally oblivious to her not ready to hang out. "Let's just order in and watch a movie or something."

"Yoga pants for the win," she said under her breath.

He gave her a confused look. "What was that?"

"Nothing," she grumbled, sitting next to him on the couch. She turned so her back was against the armrest so she could see at him. "What happened? What made you come here?"

"That obvious?"

She smirked. "I've known you my whole life. You never bail on a chance to go out. What's up?"

"My mom thinks I'm not staying at her house because I'm so promiscuous I can't go a week without getting my dick wet."

"Little do they know the truth of your current situation," she said, trying to make him smile.

"I have a well-deserved reputation, I get it, but even my mom believes all the noise about me sleeping around? I told her I was staying at the hotel because of work, but I doubt she believed me. Why should she? In the past, if I had an extended stay, I did get a hotel so I could fuck whoever I wanted without worrying if my mom would walk in. I never stay with her and Mark. I feel like a piece of shit. Something has to be wrong with me." Nate closed his eyes for a second, making Samantha's heart ache for him.

She gently rubbed her hand on his arm. "Natalie misses you, just like we all do. Knowing her, she wants to spend as much time with you as she can possibly get. I wouldn't blame her for that. We all want your time whenever you visit. Try not to take it to heart. And when it comes to sex, who cares what you do? You're single, and there's nothing wrong with that."

"But I'm not single." There was a distant sound to his voice, as if he couldn't believe the words he spoke.

This was uncharted territory.

Samantha wasn't sure what to say. Instead of words, she scooted closer to him and rested her head on his shoulder. His arms came around her, squeezing her in a snug side hug. They stayed close to each other, neither saying a word, holding on tight like it was a lifeline.

Finally, Nate spoke up. "Let's order pizza and watch a movie."

The way he sat up with his back poker straight, it was a signal the sentimental moment was over. Which was fine with Samantha. It wasn't like they were trying to fix Nate's need to be single. But she could tell the intimacy of holding each other for comfort was too much for him.

"Let me grab us some beer." She got up and scurried off to the kitchen.

When she came back, Nate put his phone on the coffee table. "I ordered the pizza."

She sat next to him and grabbed the remote control. Turning on Netflix, she put on *Schitt's Creek*. By the time pizza came, they were each a couple beers in, laughing their asses off at the show. Every episode was funny. It was like holding onto each other earlier had never happened. Just like their kiss two weeks prior. They just continue to pretend anything that mirrored a relationship hadn't happen.

Which was fine.

Really.

CHAPTER 10

SAMANTHA WOKE UP on the couch. Who hadn't fallen asleep watching TV in their living room? This time around, however, her head was in Nate's lap, her mouth particularly close to a giant banana in his pants. She sat up to put some space between them. While they hadn't discussed her face being in close proximity to his manhood, she had a feeling it would be frowned upon. They'd banned kissing, a blow job was definitely off the table.

Nate could sleep through a marching band parading by him, so he didn't flinch when she scooted away from him and his hand slipped off her back. He was stretched out, his head resting on the back of the couch.

Walking into the kitchen, Samantha decided to make breakfast. Her cooking skills were limited to toasters, microwaves, and anything grab and go, which didn't leave much room to impress. Not that she was searching for a way to wow Nate, but if he didn't like bagels, he wasn't eating.

When the fourth bagel popped, Nate lazily came into the kitchen, still wearing his jeans and t-shirt from the night before.

"Do you want to change into something else? I'm sure I

actually have some of your sweatpants somewhere in my dresser," Samantha offered.

He lifted a shoulder dismissively. "Nah, you can keep them. I'm going back to the hotel to get some work done."

"Well, you're in luck either way," she responded, showcasing her hands over the breakfast options like she was a *Price is Right* model. "I made bagels. And the real treat, I had blueberry *and* plain. You're welcome, my friend."

He cringed for a second, but this was his second time in weeks sleeping on a couch. Poor thing had probably pulled back muscle at this point.

With the plate of toasted bagels in one hand, butter, cream cheese, and knife in the other, she guided them to her dining room table. They both sat down and began eating.

Nate put his bagel down and stared at her.

"What?" She wiped her face with the back of her hand. "Is there butter on my face?"

He shook his head. "I don't even know how to have this conversation."

Yikes, that seemed way too serious for seven in the morning.

"If this is about my cooking skills, you've known for a very long time this is my finest bagel making to date," she said, a pretend sternness in her voice while pointing at her bagels, which were thankfully not burnt.

This made him laugh. "Yes, I was there for the great brownie explosion when we were fifteen."

She swallowed a bite of her bagel while groaning. "I will never live that down. Whatever you have to tell me can't be worse than that. What's up?"

He paused again.

"Last night, I vented about my mom then shut down any more conversation about it."

She shrugged. "It's okay. You and I both aren't great at the whole expressing our feelings thing. No worries."

"Do you ever think, though, maybe that's part of my problem? Lately, I've been off, like I need something more, but I don't know what it is." His gray-blue eyes penetrated hers like she had all the answers.

"I get it. For me, sometimes there are little reminders of how maybe I need something else too." She neglected to mention the whole pending annulment being her biggest reminder. It made her yearn to have someone to come home to. Like how Charlotte and Rafe's wedding made her realize how much she wished she'd found her person the way they had, the one who just got her.

"You just ignore the reminders and don't make a change?" His question wasn't meant to be a dig, but it did hurt a little bit.

She took the last bite of her bagel to buy herself more time.

Nate kept talking without touching his food. He must have had a lot on his mind. That, or with the memory of her past baking skills, he was too nervous to eat. "I think expanding business out here would help. Not only would it be more of a challenge, but I'd be here...well, not here in your apartment, but you know what I mean. I'd be back home. Maybe being close to home will fill the void."

Cue her notorious humor to lighten the mood. "Or I could step up my game and be more of a challenging wife. Like demand a delivery of flowers every day."

"You've hated flowers since you were a kid." Nate smeared some butter on a bagel. "I sent you flowers when you passed your driving test and got your license. You complained I gave you a gift you had to take care of."

This was true, but in her defense, why hadn't he just taken her to Taco Bell or bought her some candy?

"And I forgot to water them and they died awfully quick." Samantha angled her head to the side.

Nate bit his lip for a second. "I'm stressed. I don't like feeling like I'm missing something but don't know what it is."

She had no idea how to handle the complexity of their discussion. It was a serious, which she was able to do, but the only way to make Nate get out of a rut was laughter. "So far this morning, we've discussed my lack of cooking skills and how I don't like flowers. Oh, and I woke up with my mouth way too close to your banana. It almost poked my eye out. I would say, my morning has been a bit more stressful than what you're talking about."

His laughter exploded across the table. "Sammy, you always make me feel better."

"I aim to please," she told him with some sass as she cleared their plates from the table. Since her mission to make Nate smile was complete, she had to get ready for work.

He followed her into her bedroom. She stepped into her closet to change so he didn't see her undress and heard Nate flop onto her bed.

"I feel like we need to talk about my banana and your mouth a bit more." His deep voice taunted her from the other side of the closet.

It made her fumble a bit, but it wasn't like he could witness her fidgeting over his words. She quickly pulled a pale-yellow dress on before opening the door.

As she'd thought, he was laying on his stomach on her bed, playing on his phone.

"If I wanted to talk about your banana and my mouth, you would have had a better morning than just bagels," she told him while stepping in the bathroom connected to her bedroom. She scrubbed her face, brushed her teeth, and styled her hair into a low ballerina bun.

He grinned like the Cheshire cat when she came back into her bedroom. "Are blow jobs now a topic of discussion?"

"Zip it," she reprimanded him. "What are your plans the rest of the week?"

"I'm working during the day all week and plan to do lunch

with my mom, but no plans outside of that," he informed her. "I figured I would just be spending time with my lovely wife."

She slipped on her nude flats and leaned over Nate, giving him a quick kiss on the cheek. "Yes, we have marital duties this week. Let's just plan to do dinner every night, unless you have something else come up. Just text and let me know. I have to go, so just lock up when you leave."

He nodded and went back to his phone. Samantha hustled out of her bedroom before she got all daydreamy staring at Nate. It was funny. He'd initially wanted to talk about how he needed a change, and it only made her want one too.

A change that involved the two of them together.

When Samantha got to work, her day was more meeting driven than expected, which was fine with her. It kept her busy. She got a text from Charlotte inviting her to happy hour and gladly accepted. Not only because she loved wine and her friend, but it was a chance to get some breathing room from her husband.

She giggled for a second. She'd never thought that was something she would say. Let alone with Nate being her husband.

Ever since they'd gotten hitched, things had changed. Everything was different. Whenever she looked at him, she wanted to rip his clothes off. He had turned into the sexiest man she had ever seen, like she was now able to acknowledge all thoughts she'd pushed away about him.

This morning, she'd watched him sleep for a minute, adoring how he had a mischievous look about him even when he wasn't awake. She loved his shaggy hair and wanted to run her hands through it.

And that banana in his pants...it only egged her on more to see him sans clothes.

All this was just physical. Nate was a fantasy she could dream about but not actually touch. Especially after their kiss in

New York. She wasn't an idiot. If they did go past second base, it would ruin all the intangible between them. From knowing their best accomplishments and biggest fears, to being the person they each relied on and kept all their secrets. Without any doubt, she'd lose her best friend if they ever crossed the line. It would ruin everything.

But it was getting harder and harder to remember that.

WHEN SAMANTHA LEFT, Nate hung around her apartment for another hour. It wasn't like he was creeping around or anything, but she had the most comfortable bed. The only reason he got up, other than needing to get some work done, was because her soft mattress made him think of everything he could do to her on it.

They were walking a thin line from scrapping the rules and finally fucking each other's brains out. Or at least he was. From their kiss to him jerking off to visions of her more times than he'd like to admit, he hadn't been able to stop thinking about her. He'd had to lay on his stomach when she'd been changing, for fuck's sake. He'd gotten so damn hard knowing she was taking off her clothes on the other side of the closet door.

He hadn't had to deal with a random hard-on since he was in high school.

Now, it was whenever Samantha got too close to him.

Which was a nightmare.

Nate was back at his hotel around ten and got to work. He responded to emails, made appointments to walk through homes in the area, then he updated his schedule in New York to make up for anything he was missing while in California. Once he hung up with a realtor, he noticed it was almost five. Outside of lunch with his mom, he hadn't moved from the desk in his hotel room.

His phone beeped. It was a text from Rafe.

Heard you're home. Meet us in thirty at The Patio.

Rafe was direct and right to the point, which he appreciated. Happy hour sounded like fun, and since he didn't have concrete plans with Samantha, it wasn't like he couldn't see her afterward and they could grab dinner then.

Besides, after he'd left her apartment, a little space was needed. It was too easy being married to her.

It was stressful being mistakenly married to your best friend.

He was well-aware he sounded like a crybaby. He was married to a smoking hot woman who was one of the smartest people he knew and had a killer sense of humor. But all the tension between them was like a live wire. It was hard to breathe like a normal person around her.

Topping that off with the fact that he had started jerking off to her, it all seemed like some fucked up world he was living in. A night with some friends would be a much-needed distraction.

He texted Rafe back, confirming he would be there. Then he saved his work, shut off his computer, and quickly changed.

By the time he got into the rental car, he was wondering if Samantha would be there too. It wasn't like they didn't share the same friends. He was glad he'd showered and changed, not that he had to impress her.

Not at all.

CHAPTER 11

THE PATIO WASN'T crowded for five-thirty. Nate quickly found Rafe sitting at a table outside. This was the first time Nate had been to this bar, and the atmosphere was relaxed in an outside environment. Rafe picked a shaded table in the corner against a high, wooded fence. The seats were reminiscent of patio furniture, and the table had tea lights scattered in the middle. Nate waved to his friend and slid onto the empty bench.

"This seems like a table for ten," Nate said when he got comfortable. "Who else is joining?"

Rafe lifted a brow, as if he was surprised. "Charlie will be here soon."

Nate snickered at Rafe's use of his wife's childhood nickname. They all knew she hated being called Charlie. Rafe was the only one who got away with it.

"Don't laugh. She secretly loves it," Rafe responded. "Gabriella said she's coming with one of her friends from work. Tina, I think her name is. Samantha will be here. Oh, and Jason too. He mentioned he invited some people, so I figured the bigger the table, the better."

"Look who got so responsible," Nate joked with him.

Rafe smiled like life couldn't have been any better. "Marriage has that kind of effect on me. I know you swear it will never happen to you, but if you decide to settle down one day, you'll love it."

Nate stalled, wanting to tell his friend the truth. He *was* married, and he had no clue what to do about it.

A laugh made him look up as he watched Charlotte sit down next to Rafe. She kissed her husband, then asked, "What were you saying to Nate?"

She giggled as she cuddled up to him. At first, it was odd to see them together, mostly because they'd hated each other for so many years, but now, it all made sense. They were meant for each other. He had never seen either one of them so damn happy.

"If you kiss my sister in front of me," Jason joined the table, putting Charlotte between Rafe and him, "all my drinks are going on your tab."

"Should we not tell him what happened in his guest room last weekend?" Rafe pretended to whisper to Charlotte, but he was loud enough, they all heard him.

Jason pretended to gag as Gabriella and her friend showed up. Rafe had been right. The friend's name was Tina. If Nate hadn't been conflicted with the emotional turmoil he had over his best friend, he would have been all over Tina. She was blonde and curvy, and many people had already turned their heads to check her out, including Jason.

Jason was like a moth to a flame whenever a hot woman was concerned. Rafe and Nate shared a look and an eye-roll knowing their friend was about to shamelessly flirt with Tina for the remainder of the night. Gabriella stared at Jason, shaking her head no.

"I already warned her about you," she said sternly as she sat down.

That didn't deter him. He gave Tina a lazy smile. "Then I assume you know how wonderful I am?"

Tina laughed, but she didn't give in to his bait. She sat next to Gabriella, and they perused the wine list. This was right up Gabriella's alley since she worked at a winery. Everyone was ordering drinks when one of Jason's friends arrived.

He must have just left a corporate office because he wore a suit and had his briefcase with him.

"Thanks for letting me crash," he announced, sitting next to Jason. "My name is Roberto."

Before Nate could introduce himself, Samantha came running to their table. Her cheeks were flush, her dark hair swishing back and forth.

"Why are you running like there's a fire?" Charlotte asked her as Samantha sat down in the empty seat next to Roberto.

Samantha chuckled even though she seemed out of breath. "I think their happy hour prices end at six. I was busting ass to get here for a three-dollar glass of wine."

Roberto gave her a smile. "You ran for a bargain glass of wine?"

She returned his smile. "Priorities, right?"

Everyone around them was talking, except Nate. He clenched his beer as he watched this guy they all just met show interest in Samantha. It wasn't like he hadn't seen this before. Fuck, in the past, he'd even helped be her wingman. But that was when she'd been single.

Samantha wasn't single.

A wave of anger washed over him, and he glared at her. She smiled, she laughed, she even touched the guy in the suit's arm. Nate felt like something was constricting around his neck, like he couldn't breathe.

He stood up abruptly and stormed off to the bar.

There was no way he could watch her get hit on without

wanting to scream, *"She's mine and we have a court order to prove it."*

ROBERTO IN THE expensive suit was laying it on pretty thick. Poor guy had no idea she wasn't going home with him, but there was nothing wrong with having a little fun. Besides, he had a lilt of a Spanish accent, and who didn't love an accent?

He was hot. Gabriella and her friend were both eyeing him up.

Samantha was ready to get her flirt on. That was, until her stupid husband stood up, almost knocking his chair over, and stomped off to the bar.

They still had eight more weeks of pretend marriage. If he kept this up, two months were going to be brutal.

"What does your job as a social media consultant entail?" Roberto asked, leaning closer to her.

She loved her job and could talk about it all day. Unfortunately for her, she had another man to deal with.

Tilting her head at him, she gave a teasing smile. "Let me go grab a drink at the bar, then I can tell you all about it."

Roberto grabbed at his chest, like his heart was aching. "Ah, a blow off."

He made her laugh. She shook her head no, denying how she was actually shutting him down, even though that was the case.

"But you have a drink," he told her, holding on to her hand as she stood up.

She gave him a regretful smile. "I have a feeling I'm going to need more than one."

He glanced at the bar, then back to her, as if he figured out the reason for her departure was the man stewing at the bar. It was her cue to leave the table. She headed to the bar where Nate stood all by himself.

While he wasn't loud and boisterous like Jason, Nate was hardly ever alone. Women flocked to his dark and mysterious look. But he was definitely giving off the vibe of *proceed at your own caution*. This was a new side to him, and she wasn't sure she was a fan.

Standing next to him, she tapped her hip to his. "What's wrong?"

He turned to stare at her. His piercing grayish-blue eyes were swimming with anger. Samantha lifted her nose up with annoyance. Nate and his bad attitude needed to stop.

"Answer me," she pushed. "What's wrong?"

"What's wrong?" he said through a clenched jaw. "I guess you could say I'm not fond of watching my wife flirt with anything that has a dick."

"Are you kidding me?" she whisper-yelled.

His eyes never left hers. "Does it sound like I'm joking?"

"No. It sounds like you're jealous," she snapped.

Nate's hand dragged through his hair. "There's no way I'm jealous."

"Really?" she shot back. "Let me remind you how you're the one freaking out because another man is talking to me."

"Is it really horrible of me not to want you blatantly flirting with other men in front of me?"

This reaction from him made her pause. It seemed like he cared, which was so far from anything he'd ever said he wanted before—let alone with her.

"That goes against the rules," she gently reminded him.

The rules were there to protect them. With Nate's struggle with jealousy and her ongoing confusion of wanting him, it was like they were sailing on a sinking ship. She clutched to those rules like a life vest.

"**FUCK THE RULES**," Nate responded with heat.

This was taking a turn. Sure, a demanding and angry Nate when he was going all alpha was hot as well, but his behavior needed to be in check. The rules he helped make, he was disregarding all of them because some guy was flirting with her. None of this made sense.

"Nate..." Samantha was going to reason with him. If he kept acting like this, he was destined to regret it. She didn't want him to confuse this façade of a marriage for something real. Not when he'd made it perfectly clear it wasn't what he wanted.

"Samantha..." His tone was nothing but serious.

Her hands were on her hips, her eyes narrowed. "It goes without saying you're acting like an idiot."

The bartender interrupted them to see if they wanted another drink. Without taking his eyes off her, Nate handed his credit card to the bartender and asked him to close out both their tabs. The bartender must have sensed the tension because he didn't say much, but she heard him call out to their waiter.

"We're leaving," he told her through a clenched jaw.

That was it. Two demanding words expecting her to follow his lead. He must have bumped his head on something earlier in the day if he actually believed she was going to up and leave all because he had a piss poor attitude.

"No," she said flatly, her hands still on her hips and nose in the air.

Nate leaned down and whispered in her ear. "I don't remember it being a question up for debate. Meet me out front."

Goosebumps traveled all over her body at his warm breath on her skin and bossy declaration. He took a step back, signed their tab the bartender left on the bar, and walked away. Samantha was transfixed. She had never been into a man who was challenging and possessive. The way things were progressing with Nate, though, she was blushing, and excitement coursed through her.

She shook her head to get back to reality.

Sexy as Nate was, she wasn't a doormat.

This new game they were playing was dangerous. There was no way she was asking how high just because he'd ordered her to jump. Maybe in his past women did whatever he asked—or demanded, she corrected herself—but not this time.

Keeping her head held high, she marched back to the table.

Charlotte gave her a look like she'd seen the whole interaction. "Where's Nate?"

"He left." She sat down, drinking the rest of her wine. She wondered if Roberto had taken note that she hadn't come back with another drink, but when she turned to him, he was fawning all over Tina.

Rafe finally pulled his attention away from staring at Charlotte. Their cuteness she normally loved, but Samantha had about had it with anything having to do with husband and wife. "I can't believe he didn't say goodbye."

"Jet-lag," she assured them. While her heart was racing, screaming at her to meet Nate out front, she wasn't budging. He didn't get to flip out and order her around to get what he wanted.

Especially since she doubted either of them actually had a firm idea on anything going on between them.

The only thing she imagined they would agree on was things were swiftly changing whether they liked it or not.

CHAPTER 12

TEN MINUTES AFTER Nate's notorious last words demanding her to leave happy hour, Samantha sat with her friends, a fake smile on her face, acting like all was well in the world. She wished that were the case. Instead, she was all twisted up inside and her world was running rampant.

Her frustration with Nate was long gone. After debating why he had gone bananas, she'd become more empathetic. Like maybe this whole marriage thing was taking a larger toll on him than she'd realized. Her phone vibrated with a text from him.

Samantha, I'm on my last strain of sanity. Get your ass out here or I will cause a bigger scene than I already have.

So much for feeling sorry for him. His behavior wasn't doing him any favors. She texted him back.

This isn't a good look on you.

Mostly. His pushy attitude wasn't a good look on him *mostly*, and that was because he was confusing the hell out of her. This rollercoaster they'd been on since Vegas had one too many loops.

Everything is a good look on me.

She smirked. He was right. Still, would it kill him to use his manners?

I'm searching for the please in your texts, but I can't find it.

Per usual, she fell back on her humor. Informing Nate how he was acting like an asshole, *again*, wasn't something she was doing through text. She was a grown up, or pretending to be anyway, and denouncing his asshole commentary was best done face to face. It was her pride, however, holding her back from going out front. He deserved to sweat it out a bit.

Please, for fuck's sake, please meet me outside.

She heard the desperation through a text. Well played, Nate. Well played. She had to give him some credit.

"You've been on your phone. What stole your attention?" Jason asked, moving to sit in the empty chair next to her.

"Trust me, even if I explained it to you, you wouldn't believe me."

Jason smiled. "As long as you aren't running off to Vegas and getting married like my sister did, I'd believe you."

Oh, the irony. Samantha bit back a laugh. Another text arrived.

Please get the fuck out here and talk to me. PLEASE.

Jason chugged the last of his beer and put the glass back on the table. He shook his head in disdain. "I know that look. Another one fell in love. Absolute insanity, if you want my opinion."

Not bothering to correct him, Samantha said goodbye to everyone and left. After all, he had said please.

WHEN SOMEONE WAS about to make a mistake, it vibrated deep in their bones. Like right now, text after text, Nate acknowledged he was crossing a line. How he had been reacting to Samantha was driving him crazy. This magnetic pull to her was unexplainable. It was like Pandora's box had been opened and all the years of pushing her into the friend-zone had blown up in his face.

Fuck it, he wanted her despite the consequences.

Desperately.

Uncontrollably.

Being able to fuck his wife had taken up permanent residency in his thoughts.

He leaned against the wall on the side of the restaurant, doing his best to channel his inner patience and wait for her.

Ever since their idiot asses got married, their relationship had turned into some kind of soap opera with the rollercoaster ride it has become. One minute they were friends, the next they were mauling each other. Either way, it was like he had been waiting forever for her. Never had he been like this with a woman. Jealousy was something he'd mocked his friends for if it ever happened to them. He was more of a one-and-done kind of guy. No promises for more than just a night of orgasms.

Now, the thought of any man touching Samantha made his skin crawl.

He was irrational as fuck about it, but it didn't make a difference. All of this was fake.

"Nate," he heard Samantha call out as she left the restaurant.

His heart was racing. He pushed off the side of the wall and stepped out of the ally so she could see him.

Her smile did nothing to slow down his heart. "I love that your hide-and-seek game has not improved since we were kids. You always got impatient waiting for someone to find you and would pop out not even five minutes into the game."

He crooked a finger, urging her to get closer as he leaned against the wall again. "So, you shouldn't be surprised by my lack of patience."

Samantha joined him on the side of the restaurant and swatted at his arm. "You're right. I guess I'm more surprised about what a jealous man you are. Who knew all it took was for you to say *I do* to make you lose it?"

He grabbed her hand and turned them around so her back was now against the brick wall. There was no more playfulness with the firmness in his hold.

"Nate?" she whispered, more as a question.

Her sparkling brown eyes were wide. He rubbed his thumb along her jawline. Embracing the calm before the storm. Taking in the quiet moment because everything was about to change.

"I'm not sorry," he whispered.

She arched her head to the side. "Not sorry for what?"

His hands slipped around the back of her neck, and he felt her pulse racing under his touch. She licked her lips, and his dick got hard. Fuck, he wanted her so badly, it hurt. The *should we, shouldn't we* debate was long gone. He had to kiss her.

Nate wasn't gentle when his lips crashed down on hers, bruising her mouth with his. There was no patience as his teeth pulled on her bottom lip, demanding a reaction from her. When her mouth slightly opened, welcoming more, his tongue swiped in, possessively taking control. He had to explore every inch of her.

There was no way he could get enough of her. His hands gripped her hair, only to tilt her head up to deepen the kiss. He tasted her mouth like it was his last meal. Samantha hummed with pleasure against him.

This was the match that lit their world on fire.

Her hands wrapped around his waist, grasping at him to get closer so she could rub herself against him. Nate moved his mouth to kiss along her jaw before biting the skin below her ear. Fuck, when she moaned his name, he swore he was seconds away from coming.

There were zero fucks given about being outside. He grinded against her, kissing her so passionately, it was as if he was marking her for anyone to see. She slipped a hand under his shirt and touched all over the smooth skin of his chest. They devoured each other, tongues fighting for control. It was intoxicating. Nate was becoming unglued from every touch they shared.

His hands yanked her hair back so she had no choice but to look at him. They were both panting, sagging against each other.

The only gripe about the situation was how they were in public against a restaurant wall. Nate was desperate to rip her clothes off and sink inside her. What a joke it had been mulling over this, wondering if it was a mistake. He was ready to kiss her again—he never wanted to stop—but she put her hand over his mouth.

Apparently, she didn't want the same thing he did.

He was the one who got burned from their fire.

NO BIG DEAL. At all. She was making out with her husband against a wall, where their friends who had no idea they were married were in close proximity. What were they doing? This wasn't part of their rule book on surviving their drunk wedding scandal. She had to pull away or she was scared she would say fuck it to indecent exposure and let Nate have his merry way with her.

He rested his forehead on her shoulder.

"What the hell is wrong with us?" Nate panted out against her.

Good question. That had been on repeat ever since their first dry hump session a couple weeks ago in his apartment.

The insatiable need to rip his clothes off had spiraled out of control. Part of her wished he was an awful kisser so she didn't want to keep coming back for more. But that wasn't the case. Every time they kissed, they got closer and closer to being more than just friends. Without a doubt, if they let desire take over, the sex would be the best she ever had. But it wasn't worth the crossfire. Nate didn't do long-term.

She couldn't forget that.

"I think we're attracted to each other," she was careful with her wording because she wasn't sure what these feelings meant. She confided she also wanted him naked, but also hesitated to tell him she wanted him in a relationship. A real relationship, not fake, which she was sure would only result in a mess—one she didn't want to clean up alone. "Only because we're the only option we have, you know?"

Nate stood straight and took a step back from her. He crossed his arms and glared at her. "That's what you think? That I only want to fuck you because you're my only option? Is it impossible for you to imagine maybe I want more?"

Did he? That would be a shock if it were true.

"Nate, let's just both admit we're attracted to each other, but it's probably amplified because of our situation."

He dropped his arms, but still held the glare.

"If we go back to my place and fuck this out of our system, what happens next? Will we just be fuck buddies until we get our annulment? Or do we settle for a divorce since we consummated the marriage? Or what about when one of us gets tired of the other? What do we do then?" she rambled on, confessing thoughts that kept her up at night.

The glare dissolved. "Fuck, I didn't think of it like that."

Of course he hadn't. He wasn't thinking long-term—another reason for them to ignore the chemistry

"Let's chalk it up to we're players being benched right now and we're just desperate to play," Samantha half-heartedly told him.

He shrugged, not giving his opinion, then guided her away from the wall toward his rented car. They didn't talk much as he drove her home, and it was probably for the best.

She didn't want to make the mistake and invite him inside.

Her self-control was on its last leg.

CHAPTER 13

DESPITE THE OFFICIAL awkwardness between them, they still had a dinner date planned two days later. Communication was through text, only deciding on where to go and what time. There was a slight pang of hurt when he reminded her to take pictures so they had more evidence to show the judge. She couldn't even bring in her humor to defuse the passive aggressive messages.

Despite the glaringly obvious reasons she should have packaged her feelings for Nate and shipped them off to Antarctica, never to be found again, she still thought about the kiss.

While she was at work and responding to emails.

When she went to lunch with her coworkers.

Watching Hulu before bed.

Nate and his distracting lips were unforgettable. To make it worse, she stood in her closet, shuffling through her clothes, trying to find the perfect outfit. This was not how someone who stopped things from going further acted.

Her phone rang, and she smiled when she saw it was Charlotte. "Hey, there, sister from another mister."

Charlotte laughed. "I love how you answer the phone. What are you doing tonight?"

Ugh, she wished she could confide in Charlotte. She was her one friend who would listen, not judge, and then give sound advice. But this was subject non grata. Still, she could share something about her night.

"Getting ready for a date," Samantha said. She was desperate for some outfit suggestions. "And I have no idea what to wear."

"Where are you going? And with who?"

"We're going to Foreign Cinema. I've never been before." Samantha had been pleasantly surprised when Nate had made the suggestion. She'd figured after their make-out encounter, he'd suggest somewhere to get beer and wings.

"I haven't either!" Charlotte excitedly announced. "What number date is this? Is it too soon for Rafe and me to crash?"

She chuckled, imagining Nate's face if Rafe and Charlotte surprised them for an impromptu double date.

"It's way too soon."

"Hmmm, but this man obviously means something if you're going to such a fun date spot. Did you pick the spot?" Charlotte questioned.

Samantha shifted through the dresses in her closet, nowhere closer to being ready. "No, he did. And before you ask, I'm not telling you who's taking me."

"I get it. You don't want to jinx it," her friend agreed. "I've been there, married that."

"No, no, no," Samantha said quickly. "We are nothing like you and Rafe."

Other than the whole Vegas wedding thing.

"Sure..." Charlotte sounded skeptical.

"We aren't."

"Okay."

"Seriously, it isn't like that."

"Then why are you freaking out over what to wear?"

"Zip it," Samantha said, trying to sound laidback but still fumbling over her attire.

Charlotte laughed again. If only she knew how not funny this was. "Don't go overboard. Where a sexy shirt and jeans."

Those words had her stopping in front of her silk, black, off-the-shoulder shirt.

"You're a genius! I'll do that and promise to tell you if the restaurant is worth the visit." She took the shirt of the hanger and left the closet.

"Sounds good," Charlotte told her. "And I better hear about the man too. Trust me when I say secrets just make a mess. If you like him, bring him around."

Samantha was nonchalant in her response because Nate was already around. It was already messy. On a positive note, at least she had an outfit to wear.

THE FOREIGN CINEMA was somewhere Nate had always wanted to check out. Reviews on the place had been phenomenal, from the food to the atmosphere to the overall experience. They even had a "Foreign Cinema Day," which had to mean something.

When he arrived at the restaurant, he waited for Samantha outside. There was chatter floating through the waiting area with the light noise of the movie playing in the background.

He fidgeted with the hem of his gray V-neck shirt, a bit nervous about seeing her again. His ego had taken a punch when she'd stopped them from going any further the other night. It wasn't that he blamed her, it was that, once again, he hadn't been thinking about how having sex would jeopardize their relationship. What did hurt, though, was her declaration she didn't want to be another notch on his belt because they were destined to fail. It was like everyone, even Sammy, believed commitment was not an option for him.

Well, fuck. For a long time, he'd agreed with the sentiment. Things changed.

Maybe they had been for a while.

A group of women walked by him, and one stopped.

"Why are you all alone?" the blonde asked, shooing her friends for them to go inside.

If this had been any other time, he had to admit he would have been more than welcoming of her attention. He used to not even care about personality. She was blonde, had a nice rack, and was interested.

Now, though, he wanted to end the conversation ASAP. It was wrong to flirt with someone else, at least in his mind.

He gave a small smile. "Just waiting for someone."

That didn't deter the woman. "Anyone special?"

"I'd think so." Nate glanced at his watch. Samantha was officially late. "It's my wife."

"How long have you been married?"

What in the fuck was this? He was married, why was she still pushing for more? It wasn't like they were going to become friends.

"I'm sorry I'm late." Samantha wrapped her arm around his waist as she joined him.

He looked at her, hoping to everything holy she understood this wasn't him picking someone up. In an instant, she gave him a reassuring smile that all was well.

"Who's your friend?" Samantha asked, her voice not as sweet.

Nate kissed the top of her head, playing up the husband-and-wife act. "Not sure. She asked who I was waiting for and now you're here."

Finally, the woman took a hint and left, not bothering to introduce herself.

When they were alone, Samantha let out her laugh. "Lesson

learned. I can't be late or my husband will get hit on by another woman."

He grinned. "If it counts, I learned that same lesson about you earlier in the week."

"Ah, yes, when you went all caveman on me."

Desperately, he wanted to remind her how much she'd enjoyed the way they'd kissed and made-up afterward but decided against it. It seemed like every other hang out had been filled with tension, and he needed some fun Sammy time.

"Nate." The hostess came out to them. "Your table is ready."

Samantha was giddy, hopping after the hostess to their table outside. Her excitement was contagious. He loved how animated she got, even over the small details like the hanging lights. Each day that passed, Nate was becoming more and more addicted to her.

"HOW HAVE WE never eaten here before?" Samantha asked as she stuffed, as elegantly as possible, another bite of the Pavlova dessert into her mouth. "Seriously?"

He grabbed his fork to swipe some of the peach sorbet off her plate before she ate it all. "I have no idea, but we'll definitely be coming back."

"This meringue is the best thing I've ever put in my mouth," she said with a moan.

"There are so many dick jokes I could say." He shook his head. "But we've had a good night, and I don't want to ruin it."

They'd had a great night. There was no talk of their smoking hot kisses. Instead, they'd laughed over work stories and family history while catching scenes of *The Devil Wears Prada*, which was the movie playing on the big projector. This restaurant deserved more than its own day recognized by the city, which Samantha found out was September eighteenth. Her goal was to celebrate it every year, just like Fourth of July and Thanksgiving.

"You have to say one now," she urged him.

Nate arched an eyebrow in disbelief. "The last time we had a dick situation, you shut me down and didn't talk to me. Are we saying dick jokes are on the table now?"

"Shut up." She laughed. "You know damn well the only reason I stopped us from going further was because of all the damage control it would require."

"But are you saying kissing is okay if it doesn't lead to sex?"

She was close to climbing over the wooden table to get to him for more of his kisses. Public displays and all. Kissing Nate was the best thing she'd ever experienced.

"Perhaps," she said coyly. "Only if your dick jokes make me laugh."

"You think that meringue is the best thing in your mouth, wait until you pair it with my cock."

Her laughter was uncontrollable. Kissing Nate was amazing, but it was hard to take him serious as a dirty talker. Because...well, because it was Nate.

When their waiter came over, he paid the bill. Once it was just the two of them at the table, he shot her a cocky grin. "You do realize this means you put kissing back on the table."

Thank God for that. And all it took was a dick joke.

CHAPTER 14

FIVE WEEKS UNTIL annulment day. When they'd first received their court order, Samantha had figured she'd be planning a party to celebrate the end of their sham. This imaginary party had included champagne, her friends, and a plethora of men so she had her choice of who she wanted to bring home—sex would be something she could enjoy again.

Now, though, the idea of another man touching her tasted like vinegar. The only man she wanted was Nate. Which was ironic since they were technically married and could have had a field day with each other. She had to constantly remind herself their chemistry wasn't real.

But, if it wasn't real, why was she still pissed kissing was back on the table yet they hadn't come close to doing it?

"Sammy, do you think it's too much lace?" Charlotte asked, bringing her out of her Nate-induced daze. "I don't want the material to be all anyone notices. It will be tacky."

She, Charlotte, are Gabriella were out together, putting together ideas for Charlotte's reception. After all the excitement about her and Rafe getting married in Vegas had leveled out, their parents went nuts over the fact that no one had been there to witness the ceremony.

To meet halfway, they'd decided to have a reception, inviting their family and friends, but they weren't re-doing the ceremony. Charlotte and Rafe had decided to keep that just between them. Which, Samantha had to admit, was super romantic.

"Tacky like a Vegas wedding." Gabriella laughed, nudging Samantha over her funny joke. Samantha faked a laugh. The reality of eloping sat way too close to home for her.

The smile on Charlotte's face was enough to shut them both up.

"It was perfect for us," she blissfully said. "Rafe and I haven't done a single traditional thing in our relationship, so why would we have a traditional wedding? What we did was the best."

"Well, in that case, no, it isn't too much lace. You love the tablecloths, so who cares what everyone else thinks?" Samantha answered, a bit envious of the happily-ever-after Charlotte was getting compared to her pending annulment.

Gabriella was looking through the pamphlet Charlotte had created of all the choices at the venue. Charlotte was so type A, it was surprising she hadn't laminated them.

"I definitely like that you guys are doing tapas served throughout the night," Gabriella said. "It's different and fun. Are you going to throw a bouquet or garter, any of the traditional stuff?"

"Nope," Charlotte informed them. "We aren't even having a cake. Instead, we're having a dessert table."

"Yummy!" Samantha added, because who didn't love chocolate?

"Exactly," Charlotte high-fived her. "Okay, ladies, last question. Should we have assigned seating or let everyone do their own thing? There are more than enough seats, and there are high-top tables too. Since we aren't doing a standard dinner hour because food will be constantly served, I'm torn."

The three of them sat in silence for a moment.

"I say screw assigned seats," Samantha said, speaking first. "People will like being able to do their own thing. This is more like a party."

She laughed loudly. "Those were Rafe's thoughts on it too."

"As we can see by the highlighted section on page four," Gabriella teased.

"You love my organization," Charlotte responded. "Okay, wedding details finished. What is everyone doing this weekend?"

Gabriella rubbed her hands together in excitement. "At the winery, we're having a members-only party to try a new red blend. It's dry, but oddly sweet. I can't wait to hear what the tasters think. To me, it's our best blend yet."

"You better bring us bottles," Charlotte warned.

"Obviously," Gabriella agreed. She always had them trying new wines from the vineyard where she worked, it was to the point Samantha wasn't sure if she had any other bottles at her house. "What are you doing, Samantha?"

"I'm going to New York." It wasn't a big deal, so she continued reading through the binder of reception details from Charlotte.

"Again?" Gabriella asked.

Charlotte plopped her hand on the page Samantha was reading to get her attention. "Didn't you just go, like, three weeks ago?"

Shit.

Her friends were way too observant. She had to abort this conversation.

"I did, but he has..." she paused, trying to think of a plausible excuse. "Nate has tickets to a new club opening. You know I can't pass up a chance to get dolled up and shamelessly flirt with New York's hot, single men."

Charlotte eyed her suspiciously before removing her hand

from the book. "Well, make sure you remind him to block off the weekend of the reception."

"Sure thing." Samantha was ready for a conversation change. "Wait, did you pick out invites? You have to show them to me."

And just like that, the discussion of Nate was dropped.

IF HE DIDN'T answer his phone, she was prepared to leave the message as urgent. Their friends seemed on to her. This was an SOS.

"Hey." Nate was out of breath when he answered. "What's up?"

Hmmm, a winded Nate sounded sexy. For a minute, Sam wondered if that was how he talked after sex. He was delicious.

Wait, what was he doing to sound like that?

"Samantha, are you there?" he asked, since she had yet to say anything.

"You sound like you're in the middle of...something."

There was a soft chuckle on his end. "Is my wife getting jealous?"

"No," she answered way too fast.

"Well, rest assured, I'm at the home gym. Everything okay?"

Aside from the embarrassment creeping up on her, maybe. Ugh, she had to focus on the real problem.

"I was with Charlotte and Gabriella today."

She heard him say goodbye to some people as he left the gym in his apartment building. "Nice. How's Charlotte with planning a reception? I imagine she's going spreadsheet crazy."

"Not as bad as you'd expect. I think Rafe is rubbing off on her."

"So, she doesn't have the day planned minute by minute?" Nate asked skeptically.

He had a valid point. "Okay, so she did make color-coded binders for us, but she wasn't stressed. All in all, it wasn't bad."

"Then why do you sound like Doom's Day is approaching?"

She ran her hand through her hair. "They're catching on to us."

"Meaning?"

"Meaning they're asking why I'm going to New York so much to see you. Maybe Gabriella hasn't picked up on it, but Charlotte gave me the look. Like she isn't buying my excuse."

He huffed. "Since when do you need an excuse to see me?"

"Since it's become so frequent," she informed him like he should already know. "FYI, I told them I'm visiting because you have tickets to a club opening."

"A CLUB OPENING? That was the best you could come up with?" He was annoyed she even had to give an excuse to visit him in the first place.

He and Samantha had been close friends since forever. Now, she was pressured to explain why they were hanging out. He didn't know what was worse: her making up a lie about why she was going to see him or the fact that he was offended by it.

"It's not too far-fetched. Just a couple months ago, this would have been exactly the type of thing we would have done together," she explained with a grim voice. "I hate how we have to do this, but what other option do we have?"

Perhaps, tell the truth?

He swiped away that idea immediately. Instead of making their situation worse, he changed the subject to what they were actually doing during her upcoming visit.

But no matter what he did, the nagging thought of *would it really be that awful if their friends knew?* wouldn't leave his mind.

CHAPTER 15

THERE WAS A special pep in Nate's step. It was all because Samantha's plane had landed early and she just caught a taxi to his apartment. He was ready to have some fun with her on a friend-level after her latest news of wanting to keep them a secret.

It was a reality check that this marriage was short-term.

Anything long-term wasn't for him. He'd always known this, but the craziness of them being married was making him contemplate whether he wanted more. Which was ridiculous, obviously. It was time to go back to the rules and just have some fun with his best friend. He missed hanging with her.

Samantha hadn't gotten off track, so he shouldn't either.

A knock on his front door alerted him she'd arrived.

He opened the door. "Was that Lady Gaga you were tapping?"

"Obviously." She smiled as she walked in. "Poker Face is such a fun song. I'm setting the mood for our weekend."

He pulled at her hair that was in a high ponytail, and she lightly swatted him.

Grabbing her duffle bag, he walked into his bedroom, put her stuff on the dresser, then turned to her as she followed him into his room. "Tonight, I figured we could go out for dinner then grab drinks somewhere."

"So, the norm," she added, moving her hands like shooting guns.

She was such a nerd.

"Yes, cowgirl, the norm. I figured we could just play it by ear tomorrow."

She sat on his bed, and if she were anyone else, he would have been all over her. Who had any right to be so fucking sexy after traveling on a plane for five hours? Her messy ponytail, leggings with a sweatshirt that hung off her shoulder, and fresh face were hot as hell. He put his hands in his pockets so he could resist the urge to touch her—to give in to all the damn wet dreams he'd been having. All starring her.

"It's almost seven," she informed him after looking at her cell phone. "I can be ready for dinner around eight."

This seemed like an ask to give her some personal space to get ready. He left the room and sat on his couch, waiting for her.

He could have easily done some work. Owning his own business, there was always something for him to do. But he was too distracted. Even Candy Crush couldn't occupy him. Not when she was changing in his room, taking off her clothes.

No, this wasn't about getting laid. This was about getting back to normal with his closest friend.

"Where are you whisking me away to?" she asked, walking into the room.

He stared her down. Samantha had curled her hair and was wearing jeans, some silky black shirt, and caramel-colored boots that came up to her knees. As he'd expected, she was not going to make it easy on him. Ever since they'd gotten hitched, he seemed to be constantly reminded of how sexy she was. It was getting harder and harder to ignore the attraction as well. Pun intended.

"I figured we could go to Kelly's. It's a low-key, Irish pub in the village where we can have a few drinks." He stood up, putting his phone in his pocket.

She clapped with excitement. "That's perfect. I've never been before, and we can just come home after. I'm a bit zonked after the plane ride."

They walked out together and took the elevator down to the lobby.

"Are we walking or taxi?" he asked.

"Taxi," she answered, pointing to her boots. "The heels on these would kill my feet."

Nate laughed, hailing down a taxi. It wasn't busy, so he was able to catch one quickly.

He helped her in and told the driver where to go, then he turned his attention back to Samantha. "Why bother wearing them?"

She bopped him on the nose with her finger. "Because they tie the whole outfit together, duh."

"Your inner marketer coming out, I see.

KELLY'S WAS THE quintessential Irish pub. The walls were dark brown with splashes of green on the trim. There was mahogany paneling on the lower half of the walls, and signs of Irish sayings like *"Slainte"* and *"Beauty is in the eye of the beer holder."* Different rugby and soccer club paraphernalia filled the empty spaces. The décor made her smile.

"What's the grin for?" Nate asked once they got a table.

She pointed to the framed photo near where they sat. "How can you not smile when you see the saying *'A bird never flew on one wing'*? It's basically demanding a two-drink minimum."

"At least we're good for it. We always have two drinks. One for the wait," he started.

"And one for the food," Samantha finished.

It was as if the motto they'd created when they were

twenty-one was enough to summon the cocktail waitress. They ordered Guinness and two appetizers. Within minutes, their beers arrived. They clinked their glasses for a makeshift toast.

"How's work?" Nate asked.

"Great." She was full of cheer. "My latest design for the new credit card is right on target. Creating a brand from the ground up is one of my favorite things about marketing for social media. Release date in still sixty days out, but it takes time to implement. What about you?"

"No complaints. My team delivers on time and clients are happy."

"What's missing?" Samantha immediately knew something was off with his response. He loved his job, but his tone didn't sound like it.

He took a gulp from his drink. "You know that's the same question I've been asking myself for a few months. Work and women were all I needed, but it hasn't been enough lately."

Ugh, same for her. Not that she was going to steal his thunder and complain about how her casual encounters with men had lost its allure, but she understood where he was coming from.

"Maybe you need a hobby?" she suggested. A hobby wasn't the same as an orgasm, but it was something to fill the time.

His eyes narrowed. "What type of hobby are you suggesting? My favorite activity was making a woman orgasm."

She felt her skin get red as she blushed. Luckily, their waitress came over to drop off the Rueben nachos and cheese pretzel bites. They also ordered another round of drinks, following their silly two drink rule.

"I don't know. Maybe you could grow a garden or something?"

He rolled his eyes, not impressed with the idea of fresh tomatoes from his patio. It made sense. She wasn't sure who even had a garden in the city. The food smelled so good, she turned her direction to their appetizers.

As soon as she bit into a nacho, she moaned. "This is delicious. So good in fact, I'm mad this is the first time you're bringing me here. I didn't even know I liked Reuben, let alone on the sacred nacho. I could eat this all by myself."

He scraped some nachos onto his plate.

"Smart move." She winked at him.

Their drinks arrived, and they did another quick toast.

"In my defense," Nate said between bites of food, "when you visit, it's normally so we can go to a club or party, not chill in a small pub with no chance of getting laid."

She brushed her hair over her shoulder. "Ah, before we got hitched. Truth."

"Outside of not fucking, our marriage hasn't been too bad." He gave her a lopsided grin, and butterflies swarmed in her stomach. She swatted the thoughts away of how much she loved his smile, especially when it was directed at her.

"Gee, what a compliment."

He laughed. "I know you're joking, but it really is a compliment coming from me. I never wanted any commitment, and now I see it isn't actually as bad as I imagined. We're having fun, conversation is easy, and there's no stress outside of not having sex."

She tossed him a pointed look. "Again, not the best compliment. You're pretty much saying I'm making marriage bearable."

In a sweet gesture, he rubbed his thumb across the top of her hand. Those damn butterflies were fluttering inside her again.

"You're the only person who could ever make me want to get married, Sammy," he confided in her. "That is a hell of a lot better than bearable."

That was a better response than she'd expected. Not that

the sweet words were warranted, but it beat the shit out of hearing she made marriage manageable.

"Look at you getting all soft on me," she teased, mostly to steer away from having a real conversation about their marriage. Like, seriously, what were they going to do when it all ended?

He lifted a dark eyebrow. "Is this another suggestion of yours that I need to prove to you how I'm not soft? We can leave now if you want."

Oh boy. Another round of blushing spread across her face just imagining Nate and his idea of not hard. If there was one thing completely unbearable in this marriage, it was not knowing how hard Nate could get. She had no idea what his dick felt like, and she was curious to find out. After the last time they kissed, it had been a slippery slope for her when he backed away and reminded her of the rules. It was what they needed now.

The reminder.

Of the rules.

Not of how she wanted to touch his dick.

She put on her brave face to override how badly she wanted to...well, ride him. "It was not a suggestion. In fact, we have rules in place that mandate no sex."

"Ah, how could I forget?" His smile was still in place, but the spark in his eyes was gone.

She finished her beer. "Let's blame it on the pretzel bites. Compared to the nachos, they missed the mark."

Comedic responses always worked with him. They laughed and started pointing out all the silly signs hanging in the bar while they finished their food. She snapped selfies of them drinking beer and smiling. It was back to having fun.

The desire for him still hung in the air around her, though. And she had no idea how to get it to go away.

. . .

THEY ENDED UP having a third beer before trekking it back to his apartment. Spending time with Samantha was like a breath of fresh air. She wasn't just funny, but smart and always came to him with a fresh perspective. Since they'd gotten married and were visiting each other more often, it was becoming clearer to him how important she was in his life. How needed she was. Nate would be a mess if he lost her.

He was an idiot for bringing up sex at the bar, but there was a part of him hoping she wouldn't give a shit about the rules anymore.

So much for that.

"Not to be lame, but do you care if we just watch a movie or something?" Samantha tilted her head when she asked. She was in a t-shirt and cotton shorts, which was a laidback outfit, but to him, she was good enough to eat.

"Can I pick the movie?"

"You can if we can watch it in bed. I'm exhausted."

They went into his bedroom, and it should've been like any other time she slept over, but the room was filled with so much sexual tension, it was hard for him to breathe normally. Fuck, he wanted her so badly. It was something he'd never desired before. It was like they were connected on a different level.

Samantha got on the left side of his king-sized bed and snuggled her back into the pillows. It struck him how perfect she looked in his bed. How much he wanted it to keep happening.

He shook the idea of long-term with her out of his head and climbed onto the other side of the bed. "*The Godfather?*"

"Typical." She smirked. "You're not allowed to get mad if I fall asleep."

He got closer to her and put an arm over her shoulder. "No way. You can't disrespect Don Corleone that way."

Samantha ignored his threat. "Then maybe something a little less mobster and a little more chill. What about that movie you love with John Cusack and the jacuzzi?"

"*Hot Tub Time Machine*? I thought you hated that one?"

"Which is why I won't care if I offend anyone in the movie when I fall asleep."

He reached back to his side of the bed and grabbed the remote from the bedside table. Turning on the movie, he stared at her, unsure if he should move closer again.

Rolling to her side, she looked over her shoulder at him. "I will definitely be asleep in ten minutes."

His hand circled around her waist and dragged her to him. For just one more laugh, he hovered over her and started tickling. Around her waist and ribcage were her spots, he'd known this since he was nine.

"Nate, stop it!" She laughed, screaming at the same time.

The war of tickling was on, and she was losing. Fuck, how much he loved her laughter. It was addictive to hear. "Can't make me," he sassed back.

Her brown eyes sparkled as her body shook from the tickles matched with her giggles. She looped her arms around his neck and yanked him closer to her. This move barely gave any space separating them. In an instant, the situation changed. It went from tickling in a joking manner to the chemistry crackling around them as he laid on top of her. The temptation was too much. The need was too overwhelming. The want was too desperate.

His lips dipped down, and he gently kissed her, testing the waters as to whether this was something she needed the same way he did. Her hands moved, gracing along his jaw. It was her who initiated the second kiss, as slow and hesitant as the first.

Nate was on the brink of his control snapping in half. His lips brushed against hers, this time with more pressure, before taking a soft bite of her lower lip, making her moan. Her hands crept under his shirt, sliding up and down his torso. The slow movements were excruciating since all he wanted was to rip their clothes off and finally hear what she sounded like when he thrusted inside her.

Sitting up, he yanked his shirt off. "I can't be the only topless one at this party."

"What a travesty that would be," she said with a raspy voice, then she pulled off her shirt, tossed it in the corner, and laid back topless in front of him.

He kissed her again. This time, all the sweetness disappeared as he claimed her mouth as his. She bucked her hips against his as his lips moved down her neck. Her skin was so soft, he bit down on her collar bone, sucking the mark he left on her.

"Why does this feel so good?" she moaned as he continued nibbling her neck and behind her ear.

"Fuck if I know," he mumbled back. Part of him realized he was playing with fire again. No matter what happened, he was destined to get burned. But he couldn't stop himself. "I want you, Sammy. I need to fuck you."

She arched into him while his hands traveled down her stomach.

Out of breath, she responded. "The rules. We can't."

A groan of annoyance popped out of him. He dropped his head against her shoulder. "These rules are the bane of my fucking existence."

"I don't..." she gasped as his right hand slipped under her shorts, "I don't want to fight."

Okay, she didn't want to fight. He didn't either. He'd follow her rules tonight, but he still needed to hear her come. Nowhere in the rules did it say no orgasms. It was like he won the lottery when his hand traveled under her shorts and he realized she didn't have any panties on. He stilled for a second when his fingers felt the smooth, shaved skin of her vagina. His pushed one finger inside, wishing it was his dick instead.

Samantha squirmed. "You better not stop now."

"As if I could."

His finger brushed up and down her wetness before rubbing her clit. She was so responsive as she moved against his hand for more. His thumb pressed against her, now moving in the same motion as her hips.

"Oh my god," she whispered, as if she didn't want to get loud in case it stopped the magic between them.

While his thumb never left her, his finger pushed in and out of her. He did a come-hither motion with his finger, breaking her silent streak.

"Yes, I'm close," she yelled, probably loud enough for his neighbors to hear. Not that he gave a shit. Making Samantha orgasm was his only concern.

He added another finger and kissed her neck again, making her quickly clench around him. Her back arched, her thighs quivered, and she panted as she orgasmed. It was a fucking beautiful sight for him to see.

Nate had no idea how he was going to give this up once their marriage was annulled. Going back to normal wasn't the best option to him anymore.

THE NEXT MORNING, Samantha woke up, secretly loving the weight of Nate's arm wrapped around her as they cuddled with her back against his stomach. Last night had been perfect. Sure, she was happy their friendship was tightly intact, but the orgasm he'd given her had been better than when she gave one to herself. If their commitment weren't fake, she would have classified Nate as her best relationship ever.

In reality, their annulment was rapidly approaching with only five weeks left.

Before, she would have been jumping for joy at the notion. Now, she was a bit sad at the idea her marriage was ending.

Which didn't make sense. This was all pretend, even if her feelings were starting to become very real.

"I can hear the wheels turning," Nate said groggily, rolling to his back. "What are you thinking?"

"Honest?"

"When do I ever want you to lie?"

Fair point.

"I was thinking about how we only have five weeks left to play house."

Staying on his back, he responded, "That used to seem like forever. Now, it's happening in a blink of the eye."

She couldn't have said it better.

"Does that bother you?" he asked, still staring at the ceiling.

It was her turn to roll onto her back. "Does it bother you?"

"Sammy, come on. Don't play games. Are you okay with our pending annulment?

No. No, she was not okay.

In her dream world, she and Nate could make this work. They'd already figured out how to handle long distance. Their chemistry was off the charts. Besides, they'd known each other since forever. He was her true partner.

A montage of the last two months of them feigning marriage played in her head. Of course, there were a few hiccups, but all in all, they had bonded. She'd never felt closer to anyone. Ever.

"I get it," Nate interjected, getting out of bed. "You're not hurting my feelings. We feel the same way. This was always going to be short-term. I'm getting in the shower. When we're both ready, do you want to walk around Central Park?"

She bit her lip and nodded in agreement. Not that he saw, since his back was toward her as he stomped off to the shower.

Little did he know, they did not feel the same way.

WHAT THE HELL just happened?

Nate let the hot water run down his back while he aggressively washed his hair. Last night, they made out like a couple teenagers, he fingered her to orgasm, then they wrapped up around each other when they went to bed.

Now, she wasn't sure if she was going to miss being married to him?

Those fucking rules were in place so neither one of them got hurt, but it was happening regardless. She was flying back to California tomorrow, so he was going to make the most out of today with her.

As friends.

He couldn't handle pretending anything else anymore.

CHAPTER 16

TODAY WAS RAFE and Charlotte's wedding reception. It felt like just yesterday they'd shocked the crap out of everyone when they'd announced their surprise Vegas wedding over breakfast. Samantha had literally almost fallen out of her seat. And she had been pretty sure her brother had almost choked on his omelet. Now though, she couldn't believe there was any couple as happy as them.

Clearly, her and Nate didn't count, she thought bitterly.

And it wasn't just because of the no sex rule.

She marched around her apartment getting ready, annoyed her husband seemingly couldn't wait to get their marriage annulled. It wasn't like she was daydreaming about their happily-ever-after...okay, she was, but it wouldn't taste so bitter if he actually had an emotion or two for her. Like they could go through their annulment together, both being upset.

Misery loved company and all.

The past few weeks since she'd gotten home from her last New York visit, their texting and calls had all been the same. She should have been relieved she hadn't lost him as a best friend, but she wasn't.

She slipped into her strapless champagne-colored dress that

hit above her knees. It was form fitted and had a slit on the right side of her mid-thigh. It was new, and if there were such a thing as a revenge, make-your-husband-want-you dress, this was it.

There was a blow out bar up the street from her, so her hair was in wild, massive waves. Since the dress and hair were stealing the show, she did minimal makeup and wore white heels. Her phone pinged. Her Uber had arrived, right on time. She was ready to put on her happy face and celebrate the couple in love.

When she arrived at the reception, it was everything Charlotte had planned, a mix of understated and classy touches. She found Rafe talking to his parents so she went to him for the first congrats hug.

"Sammy, you look amazing," his mom said, giving her smile.

His dad handed her a glass of red wine. "I agree. Your mom told us you've been traveling to New York a bit more. It agrees with you."

Rafe shot her a confused look.

"Oh, you know how Nate and I love to cause trouble in the city," she said off-handedly, like it was the norm. Used to be anyway. "Enough about me. Rafe, this is your night. Congrats, my friend. You and Charlotte are seriously glowing. Love looks good on you."

The goofy smile returned to his face at the mere mention of his wife. "I'm a lucky fuck, that's for sure."

"Rafe, language!" his mom reprimanded.

He gave his mom a kiss on the cheek. "Sorry, Mom."

"Samantha!" Charlotte said with excitement. "You look amazing!"

She waved her friend off. "This is about you and Rafe, not me. You're the real showstopper here. Just like I told Rafe, love looks good on you. I can't believe after all of these years you two finally got together."

Charlotte did a spin, letting the fabric around her white

dress flutter around her. "Sometimes, I'm still shocked I married my old nemesis. But I guess we knew, even as kids, we were made for each other."

Rafe pulled Charlotte against him. "Ever since our first kiss."

"No." She giggled. "Our first pact."

He gave her a kiss. "It was the kiss. Or maybe our first time—"

"Stop it right there," his father demanded. "Your mother and I don't need any more details about your firsts."

"Unless it's about the first baby." His mom winked.

Rafe and his rakish smile smirked. "I was trying to tell you about how we practice enough, but Dad stopped me."

Charlotte dropped her head into her hands. He was undeterred and kissed the top of her head. "We're married now. They know we have sex. The best," he told her, then bent down and whispered something into her ear that made her blush.

"Okay. We're going to see the other parents at the bar." His mom directed her and her husband away from the conversation —especially since it didn't bother Rafe to talk about how much he loved seeing his wife naked.

"Congrats, you two," Samantha said with envy. "Love you both."

Rafe took a moment from ogling Charlotte. "Wait, don't leave just yet. What were my parents talking about with you going to visit Nate more?"

Charlotte gave Samantha her full attention. "What is this all about?"

"It's nothing," she said, emphasizing the word nothing. "Why can't we be friends without everyone making it more?"

"Well, I'm glad you guys are just friends. My friend Whitney lives in New York and she was telling me how she grabbed lunch with him the other day. I think it was for some remodel she wants in her house, but she's interested in him. She's always had a thing for him."

"Despite Char warning her off," Rafe joked.

"Tell her I said good luck. Now, let me get a drink so I can properly celebrate my two favorite lovebirds." Samantha plastered a smile on her face, needing to get away from this situation. It was only another reminder of Nate and his ways with women. It sunk in how he was not really hers. In a few weeks, they would have no title holding each other tied as husband and wife. And little old Whitney would probably be his first escape back to his normal life of sleeping around.

"You have wine in your hand." Charlotte was suspicious of her excuse of needing another drink.

"And it's red. I don't want to risk spilling it on my dress." She put the glass on the table. "You two can get back to kissing."

She hurried off to the bar so they didn't keep asking poignant questions about her, Nate, or her drink of choice. Speaking of the devil, he lightly hip-checked her when he met her to get a drink. "Every time I look at them, they're somehow attached to each other."

Samantha looked in the direction he'd nodded, finding Rafe and Charlotte slow dancing.

"Welp, I guess that's what marriage does to you," she said, taking a gulp of the drink that matched the color of her dress.

"Not us."

She looked at him, loving the color of his bluish-gray eyes. "Ours has an expiration date."

"Which is all the more reason we should go have hotel sex." He must have pulled a card from Rafe's book. He wasn't being quiet about wanting to sleep together. Luckily, no one was around as they drifted to stand near a cocktail table.

She poised her shoulders back. "Your logic is flawed. We have rules in place, you know that."

Those eyes she loved so much rolled at her response. "Calm

down. The rules are ridiculous. I don't think they matter anymore considering I know what you sound like when you come. We both want each other. Us not acting on it doesn't protect us from shit."

"You only want me because you want to fuck." She was angry, and the tone of her voice showed it. "And I'd like to point out, you were the one who broke the rule in the first place."

"No, I didn't. If I remember correctly, kissing and touching were always on the table."

"Orgasms weren't!" she retorted, gulping the last of her champagne.

He slapped the table. "It wasn't like you said no or didn't enjoy yourself. My neighbors heard you when you came."

"Shut up."

"No. You're like a damn seesaw. By the end of the night, you're going to be wanting me again. Maybe tonight you'll let me go down on you. Do the rules allow that?"

"You're an asshole." She glared at him. "And guess what? The rules have changed. We can have sex—just not with each other!"

NATE WATCHED HER storm off, and despite wearing shoes that added four inches to her height, she was able to move surprisingly fast. Women were a rare breed—from their purses to running in heels.

He should have been grateful she'd walked away because their conversation had been bound to get worse. But when she went to the bar, it wasn't to be alone.

Nope.

She was standing next to one of Jason's friends, smiling at him like he'd invented the wheel. It was her fake smile, but the prick didn't know that. As badly as he wanted to go after her, he didn't want to cause a scene. Not at a wedding reception. Definitely not in front of their family and friends. So, he just stood there and watched her flirt, anger seething through him.

"Hey, man," Noah greeted, unaware of the hurricane building inside Nate. "How has life been?"

Still, with his eyes on Samantha, he responded, "You wouldn't believe me even if I told you."

"Doubt that. You know my twin and her stories. It's hard to shock me."

Nate didn't respond. He wasn't letting the cat out of the bag. But he was pretty certain Samantha and him being married would shock the shit out of everyone, including Noah.

"Ever since we got back from Vegas, though, she's been acting different."

"What do you mean?" He did his best to not sound too intrigued.

Noah shrugged. "You know how she loves to go out and meet people. She hasn't done that at all. I know I have a busy schedule with soccer, but when we get together for lunch, she has no outrageous Sammy stories to share. It's been weird."

"I bet."

Oh, little did Noah know the stories he could share about her.

"Anyway, I see she's back to her normal self, chatting away with some friend of Jason's. He's a player, just like...well just like how she was. I bet I'll get some story out of her soon."

"Yeah." Nate was pissed. "Excuse me."

He left the table where he stood with Noah and strode over to Samantha.

Fuck their rules and fuck her going back to her old ways.

"DO YOU HAVE plans after this?" Dimitri asked her, alluding to them leaving together.

A few months ago, she would have been all over it. But it

wasn't happening anymore. It was immature of her to have even came over and flirted with him in the first place. She'd done it out of sheer anger at Nate, which was petty. She was about to tell him she was nixing the idea of leaving together, but someone interrupted their conversation before she had the chance.

"I need to talk to you," Nate barked at her, moving to stand in front of Dimitri. Poor guy must have realized there was no chance with Nate's abrupt interjection, so he walked over to another woman at the bar. He had better luck with someone else anyway, so there were no feelings hurt on Samantha's side of things.

"And you thought interrupting my conversation with someone else was the way to do it?" she snapped back.

"Yes, in fact, I do. We're leaving," he demanded without giving her an option. "We both have rooms in this hotel. Mine or yours?"

She stomped her foot. "You've got to be joking. I am not going anywhere with you."

Nate's hand lifted her chin so she saw the severity in his face. "I'm not playing around. We need to talk. If you want to leave afterward, fine. But I'm not having a much-needed conversation with you in a reception hall where anyone can hear us."

Samantha wasn't giving in. It was like he expected her to just follow him and provide some witty comment that would bring the mood down. Not this time.

"Then I guess the conversation you think we need so badly," she used her hands to make quotation marks, "is going to have to wait."

"No."

That was his comeback. Just one solid word.

"Yes," she clipped out.

His hand moved through his hair. "Sammy, please. I'm

begging here. This shit needs to end. We have to talk about everything we've ignored."

She stepped close to him, determination in her eyes. "I have nothing to say to you. We've both made it clear nothing is happening between us."

"That's bullshit."

"You're bullshit," she swatted back, louder than she'd hoped.

"Fuck this," he said before putting the glass he held on the bar. Grabbing her arm, he started moving, and she had no option but to trail after him because the grip he had on her was strong.

She slapped his arm. He yanked her forward. He even had the nerve to say goodbye to people as they shuffled out of the ballroom. By the time they got to the elevator, he let go of her arm, and she pushed him.

"You caused a scene!" she shrieked.

The elevator opened, and he led her out. "I'll apologize tomorrow."

This was the night that broke the camel's back.

CHAPTER 17

THE TENSION WAS suffocating them.

"Why were you even talking to that douche at the bar?" Nate prodded as they walked toward his hotel room. Anger zipped through him at her being with someone else. How the hell did she not want him the way he wanted—no, needed, her?

She stopped walking, huffed and crossed her arms. "Why do you even care who I hook up with?"

He stalked in front of her, both glaring at the other. "Are you kidding me?"

"This obviously isn't a comedy act for either of us."

His hands cupped the back of her head. "You are my wife. My fucking wife. There's no way in hell I'm going to stand back and watch someone else even have the opportunity to touch you."

"What do you want from me?"

"Everything."

In that moment, in the hallway next to his hotel room door, he kissed her passionately. Wildly. Like he was afraid it might be the last time. Her hands dug into his side, yanking him closer to her. She pulled his shirt from being tucked into the waist of his pants. Then she went for the button, but he stopped her.

"As much as fucking you right here, right now, sounds amazing, let's please move to my room."

He swiped the card key, and they stepped inside his room.

"Afraid to get caught?" she taunted as she used the tie around his neck to pull him closer until her back hit the wall. His hands brushed the hair out of her face.

"Never. But the thought of anyone else seeing you orgasm makes me irrational."

With that, he kissed her again, marking her as his.

THE WAY HIS lips moved over hers, branding her with each bite, she had never been so turned on or desperate for sex. She pulled her dress up around her hips, urging him on.

"I thought you wanted to fuck me," she panted, breaking away from his kiss.

Nate took a step back, his eyes roaming all over her body. His hands grabbed each side of her thong and tugged, ripping her underwear off.

"Oh shit," she murmured. That was the first time someone had actually destroyed her underwear to get her naked. And she liked it.

They sloppily got his pants down, but only shoved his boxer-briefs low enough for his cock to pop out. Wasting no time, Nate aligned his dick with her opening and thrust inside. He stilled for a moment, and she wasn't sure if it was because he needed it or knew she did.

She was stretched to the brim.

"Samantha," he moaned before biting her neck.

Her legs were wrapped around him. He was holding her up with his hands by gripping her ass. It was primal as he pushed into her again. There was a touch of pain as he filled her, but it was sexy as hell as they fucked each other against the damn wall.

"I need to see more of you," he gruffed as he waddled over to the bed, tossing her down so he could take off the remainder of his clothes.

Samantha followed his lead and got out of her dress as fast as possible. He climbed over her and kissed her.

He nipped at all her skin, not missing a single spot. When he licked and bit the sensitive flesh under her breast, her nails scratched his back.

"Fuck me," she groaned, not wanting anymore teasing or foreplay. It had been weeks and weeks of wanting each other. Now that they were green lighting it, she had to feel him inside her, fucking her.

Nate was a good listener. His cock slammed into her, taking her breath away. His hand grazed down her body and started to rub her clit, making her close to orgasm. Her body was beginning to tighten up, but she was desperate to have some control. She moved so he rolled to his back and she got on top.

Her hips grinded into him. She was so close, her entire body was tingling. Nate must have decided he wanted control back because he lifted her off him so he could sit on the edge of the bed facing her.

"Look at us," he demanded as he moved her back into his lap. Now, her back was against him, and they both faced the hotel mirror.

He grabbed her hips, and she started grinding again once he was fully seated inside her. Her legs draped over his, and his hands held her breasts while she thrust her hips.

"Do you see how sexy this is?" Nate whispered in her ear. He kissed her neck, and her head dropped to his shoulder. "No, I want you to watch. I want you to watch me make you come."

There was a neediness in his voice. When she tilted her head back to watch them in the mirror, she saw his one hand leave her breast. His fingers slid down and brushed over her sensitive clit. It didn't take long before her body was shaking and she was crying out his name in pleasure while she orgasmed. When she stopped trembling, Nate stood up, bringing her along with him.

He took a few more hard pushes inside her before he pulled out and came all over the floor.

Samantha didn't care. That had been, by far, the best sex of her life. She flopped back on the bed, Nate quickly doing the same next to her.

She was exhausted and didn't have time to worry about what might happen the next day.

WAKING UP, FULLY sated after a night of the greatest sex of his life, Nate was on cloud nine. Part of him figured if he and Sammy had ever crossed the line from friendship to...well, to whatever they were, it would be epic. He was in bed, and he couldn't stop staring at her. She was sleeping, her dark hair swept across the pillow. Even with her light snore and a smidge of drool on her cheek, she was the best thing he had ever woke up to.

Only problem for him: was this the same for her?

She rolled to her back, slowly blinked her eyes, and smiled.

So far, so good.

"Good morning," he whispered to her.

For a second, she bit her lip, and his dick sprang to attention, ready to pounce for another round.

"Well, it was a good night," she responded, rolling her head to the side so they were looking at each other.

He nodded in agreement. "The best night."

"Most explosive night," she countered with a grin.

"Intense night."

"Mind blowing night."

"I'll agree to it all," he told her, halting the back in forth.

To him, it seemed like everything was simpatico between them, but he had to know for sure. "How are you feeling?"

"Outside of my vagina being sore," she teased, sticking her tongue out, "I feel really good."

"You're sore, huh?" There was a touch of pride in his voice. He'd made his mark on her.

She softly swatted his arm. "Yes, and you know exactly why."

Without missing a beat, he grabbed her hips and pulled her to the middle of the bed. He kissed and nipped her skin from her neck down to her breasts.

Her body shivered beneath him as his mouth explored lower, biting her pelvic bone. Finally, he got where he wanted to be. He pushed her thighs apart and stared at her vagina for a moment. Fuck, if he could, he would live in there.

He glanced up, making eye contact with Samantha. "Let me kiss her so she feels better."

Before there was a response, Nate licked her wet center. When she moaned, he smiled. He was going to give her the best oral of her life.

CHAPTER 18

IT WAS AFTER lunch when Samantha and Nate finally left the hotel bed. Or, more accurately, after they got out of the shower and put clothes on. As it turned out, if they were naked, one of them was touching the other until they couldn't take it anymore.

Then sex.

Hot, sweaty sex.

Samantha blushed at the memory of the past twenty-four hours. Somewhere in her mind, she's known if she'd had sex with Nate, it would have been the best she'd ever had. In reality, it was so much more than that. He'd ruined her for anyone else, it was that intense between them.

Nate grinned. "I have no regrets about requesting late checkout for both of our rooms since it means I get two more hours with you."

His comment popped the happiness bubble she was frolicking in. Everything with her and Nate was on some sort of timeline. Four more weeks of their sham marriage. Three more days until he went back to New York. Two more hours in the hotel. There was an exit strategy wherever she turned, and it hit her hard. She didn't want a timeline. In her fantasy world, she wanted to have Nate. Period. Not with some predetermined expiration date.

Maybe sex had crossed the line.

How was she going to go back to normal with him now?

"Talk to me," he coaxed her.

This was where she needed to rely on her humor.

"Well, I'd hate to disappoint you for the late check-out charge," she told him with a smile she was sure he could tell was fake.

He sat down on the bed and patted the space next to him. "You know I don't care about that. One minute, you're all smiles, and the next, it's as if someone stole your puppy. What's wrong?"

"I wouldn't say wrong, per se."

He took a deep breath. "Then what, per se, is it?"

She sat down in the vacant space next to him, giving them some space on the king bed. "I don't regret last night."

"That's a good start."

As he said the words, the bitter tone to them sank through. She was mucking up this conversation, but she wasn't sure how she could save herself and their friendship after what had happened.

"Hey," she said gently, "last night—"

"And this morning," he reminded her.

"Let's just say all the orgasms were great. But there's also the scene we caused, and the questions that will be asked, and most important, our friendship." She paused tentatively, afraid of the answer to the next question. "What are we supposed to do now?"

This was where she was able to give him multiple options. The most ideal was to give this relationship a chance. The least favorable was to pretend last night had never happened. She and Nate had always been two peas in a pod, known for casual relationships and good times, not marriage and forever commitments. Something in her had shifted, and it wasn't just because of the mind-blowing sex. The past two months, changing her lifestyle to illustrate to the judge they'd tried, had only proven to her how much she was actually ready for the next step in her life. After being in a quasi-relationship with Nate, it made her realize how much of it wasn't actually fake. How she was ready for more, and not with just anyone, but with him.

His silence was making her heart race.

What was he thinking?

He scratched the side of his head before looking at her. "Sammy, you have always been my best friend. If you're worried last night is going to ruin our friendship, you're wrong. I would *never* let anything come between us."

"Not even your—"

He let out a soft chuckle. "No, not even my dick could come between us, as much as he would like it."

His words were assuring, helping in calming her down. He was right. Nothing could come between their friendship. Apparently, not his dick or even her heart.

"I don't know what to do. Everything is changing, yet everything's the same," she whispered.

He cupped her face. "How about we not blur the lines right now? When our marriage is over, let's see if we still want to rip each other's clothes off or if this desire is because we're in the moment of playing husband and wife."

Right. This was all pretend to him.

"How are we going to explain our grand exit from Charlotte and Rafe's wedding?"

Nate looked up at the ceiling for a minute, his hands still holding her jawline softly. "How about we make a joke about it, like you lost a bet or something?"

"Just a drunk moment."

"A quick little argument."

"It meant nothing." Which was par for the course for them as it was.

Nate kissed her forehead before standing up. "Exactly. No big deal."

With that, he started packing up the room. "When I check out, I can take you home if you want."

"Sure," she agreed, falling back onto the bed.

It was official. This was the oddest morning after of her life. And she wasn't sure how it was going to get better for her and Nate.

BLUR THE LINES.

What a bunch of bullshit. The look on Sammy's face, the confusion and nervousness, he would have said anything to calm her down—to make sure she understood he would never not be her best friend. He'd never leave her side.

The whole blur the lines comment had only been to put her at ease. He stomped around the hotel room, smashing all his clothes into his suitcase. It was like the idea of commitment to him, outside of friendship, was enough to make her lose her cool. He stepped into the bedroom area of the room and saw Samantha lying on the bed.

Fuck, he could tell she was upset.

He would do anything for her.

Anything. Regardless of the final outcome of what happened in Vegas, Samantha was a constant in his life, and that was never going to change.

He had to stop acting like some caveman and get it together. Because he'd told her the truth. They would always be best friends.

Nate sat on the bed. She hadn't moved since he'd started packing. Her mind was probably on auto drive, freaking herself out. Perhaps a push to get packed would help her relax. "I'm almost packed. Did you want to go to your room and get your stuff?"

She sat up. "Luckily, I don't have to pack since I stayed here, but I'd love to change. If someone sees me leaving the hotel doing the walk of shame, our story of last night being a silly bet won't be believable."

Oh, yes, another lie they were telling everyone.

It was never-ending.

"How about you go to your room and we meet in the lobby in thirty-minutes?" he suggested.

Not to sound like an asshole, but some time away from her was needed, even if it was only thirty-minutes. The space wasn't just for him, she needed it too.

"That works!" she said hastily, grabbing her shoes. Before he knew it, she was out the door.

Once the door shut, he muttered, "Fuck," and sat in a random chair in the room. Instead of thinking of ways to solve the million problems brewing with Samantha, he closed his eyes and let the memory of last night take residence. Not that he would tell her, but the sex had been so hot, he jerked off to what it had been like fucking her last night. All before he had to meet her in the hotel lobby.

CHAPTER 19

THE NEXT DAY, Nate was scheduled to tour a house close to his parents, which was a big step. This was a house he had an interest to actually move into. Not that he was willing to give up life in New York, but with branching out his business and wanting to be closer to his family, it seemed like the right time.

Yesterday, after he'd dropped Samantha off, Nate had grabbed a drink with Noah. There had been no mention of him dragging Samantha out of the reception, which was slightly disappointing. Not because he didn't have to lie—who wants to do that shit?—but because no one thought anything of substance would actually happen between him and Samantha.

It was better off that way. The less people involved in their makeshift nuptials, the better. Which meant less people involved in the damage that was bound to ensue once the annulment happened.

Truth was, sex or not, the lines were blurred. He had to make sure it didn't impact Samantha. Not after he saw how conflicted she was about everything.

He pulled out his phone and called Samantha.

"Even when you're on west coast time, you forget I work," she answered with a smile.

Checking the clock, he saw it was three. "Damn, you're right. When do you get done?"

"Five, just like every other day. Why, what's up?"

"Any chance you'd be willing to leave work at four and meet me to tour a house?" There was no way he was buying a house without her opinion.

She hummed while he heard clicking on her end.

"I can," she said. "But you owe me a milkshake or something because I had to reschedule a few meetings."

"I can deliver a chocolate milkshake with whipped cream. Meet at your house in an hour then we can go?"

Samantha agreed, and they got off the phone. He was sure the anxiety was due to looking at a prospective house, a place that would be his new home. Expanding his renovation business has been a priority for what seemed like forever. Taking the steps to do it was exhilarating.

Pulling up at four, Samantha was just getting home from work. Nate bit his fist, admiring her. She was sexy as hell, confidence surrounding her in straight-legged black pants and a green blouse. If things were different between them, despite the importance of touring the house, he would have dragged Samantha inside and devoured her.

"Hey," she shouted to him. He was still in his rental car. "Do I need to change?"

No way. He loved her in work clothes because he barely got to see it. "As long as you don't spill the milkshake on yourself, you're good."

She hopped over to his car and got in. "Good, I didn't feel like changing. So, where are we headed?"

In normal fashion, it was like nothing had happened between them. He should have been grateful Samantha wasn't the type to be dramatic, but he was the one who'd said let's not blur the lines, so this was his fault.

He shook his head before answering. "I think I found a

house."

"Duh," she rolled her eyes. "Is this a new client?"

This was big news he was dropping on her. He took a quick inhale before he explained. "I think I found a house for me to move into and be here on a more permanent basis. It's about twenty-five minutes from your place, but still in Oakland."

She applauded with excitement. "This is amazing. You've been talking about the next step for your career for awhile now. I'm a bit envious of your flexibility of being able to live on either coast. While I'm excited for you and will be obsessed with you close to home, what's prompting all this?"

He turned the music down. "You know how it's been. For months now, before we even went to Vegas, something has been off. I've been in a funk. I love New York, but I need more."

She nodded her head, accepting all he told her.

He made a turn off the highway, getting closer to the house. "I guess I always imagined coming home to be like a death sentence. But the more time that passes, the more I see how much I miss out on being so far away."

"Is missing home a funk, though?" she probed.

He shrugged. "The only thing I know is something isn't right anymore. I think being home on a more regular basis will help."

They pulled into the neighborhood, and a sense of ease washed over him. If he did move back, even on a part-time basis, this place felt right. He made one more turn, then parked in the driveway. They both got out of the car.

"The roof is terra cotta." Samantha adored the front of the home. "And it's a rancher, which is great. How many bedrooms?"

"Three, but one will be an office," he said, grabbing her hand. "Let's look inside."

He took out the key the realtor had given him and they stepped inside. Nate explained how each room looked now, but what he hoped to do. The house needed work, which was why it was affordable in such a nice neighborhood. But needing work didn't deter him. It was more of a motivation factor because he loved working on houses.

"Your vision for this house turns it into a home," Samantha gushed. "I'm completely in love."

Having her onboard was going to make buying the house that much easier. He smiled.

THIS HOUSE WAS perfect. Samantha knew Nate would improve the interior within six months flat. Every room they walked into, his energy sparkled with how he imagined the room would look when he was finished remodeling.

After an hour exploring the house, they went back to the car.

"When will you put an offer on it?" Samantha asked, putting on her seatbelt.

His left hand tugged at the collar of his shirt. "Who said I was putting in an offer?"

"Um...you did when you created a whole new interior design. Nate, it's beautiful and in a great location. You should do it."

"What about you?" he countered. "You've been talking a lot recently about how much you love New York. Do you think you could have a schedule like me?"

This was uncharted territory since they'd hashed out not blurring the lines.

She laughed the idea off. "I work in corporate America. They don't care about my whimsical idea of working wherever I want."

"Please, you could market the idea to the CEO and get it."

"You have no idea how people with an actual boss work, do you?"

He switched lanes on his way back to getting to her house. "Sure, I don't know what it's like to have a direct boss, but I think the answer is easy. Are you not interested in asking because you love your job and don't want to lose it, or are you not asking because you don't like the idea of working wherever you want?"

This was Nate, boiling a problem down to its most simplistic form.

"It's not that easy."

"It is, though. What do you want in life? Once you know that, it's on you to make it happen," Nate said with confidence.

She paused. Was it that easy?

"Come on," he urged. "What is the dream of professional Samantha?"

"Okay, in a dream world, I'd be a marketing consultant helping start-up companies. This would give me the luxury of working where I want, but also being able to help the little guy in business, not the money-hungry bank. But there's too much risk involved." She had to add the last sentence because it was what she had been telling herself. It was the whole reason she hadn't made the jump.

He pulled into her driveway. She was about to get out of the car, but he grabbed her elbow to keep her in. "What's the risk?"

She faced him. "Outside of the fact that I might fail, which would be bad all on its own? I only have so much money saved up. How would I pay for all the other expenses of starting a business on my own? How would I pay rent once I run through my savings?"

"Maybe the answer is right in front of you."

"What does that mean?" she questioned.

He turned away from her. "Nothing. I'm just saying, don't give up on yourself too quickly. That's not the Samantha I know."

"Same goes for you. Take the next step, Nate. Buy the house."

She got out of the car and walked into her house. They'd had a great day, but their parting words had sounded more about them and less about their career moves. Why couldn't Nate make their growing attraction as simplistic as he made everything else?

CHAPTER 20

THERE WERE TWO weeks left in their marriage, and thoughts of it consumed most of Samantha's day. Even while she was flying across the country for another one of their scheduled visits, there was an emptiness inside her. Their new relationship status was sure to implode on them, and the worst part, was even though they knew it, they weren't in the slightest prepared for the pending destruction. Every other visit, there were highs and lows. When they took out the required court-order, would they be able to go back to normal?

Did she even want to go back to normal?

Not to say his dick was a game changer, but after they had sex, it seemed impossible to forget. Like, what kind of man was able to deliver that many orgasms? Of course, Nate was sexy as hell, smart, and goal-oriented, but now she knew he was also a beast in the bedroom.

No way was she ever going to forget that last part.

The marks from his mouth and the bruises on her hips from how passionate they were together had just recently disappeared. Kind of sad because she'd loved the memory on her skin, but it didn't matter. Nate had marked her, and now she had to deal with the aftermath.

Her plane landed with turbulence, and it was like a foreshadow of all the questions running through her head. They were wild and shaky about her future with Nate. Once she was off the plane and had her bag, she went outside to catch a taxi to Nate's place. He had a work meeting with a new client so he couldn't meet her. Which wasn't a big deal. In fact, this was more like when she would visit before they'd gotten hitched. She wondered if he'd scheduled the meeting just to get them back on the friendship track.

After the twenty-minute drive, Samantha arrived at his apartment and went inside. The first thing she noticed were the yellow roses. That was new. She laughed, prepared to tease him for his Martha Stewart décor when he got home—until she read the handwritten note next to floral arrangement.

Sorry I couldn't get you from the airport—this client is like a needy child. I promise to make it up to you.

This was yet another change. So much for Nate putting them back on the friendship track.

He'd never done romantic gestures like this before. She liked it. She leaned in to sniff the flowers, smiling the whole time. Her phone rang. It was Charlotte.

"Hey, sis with a different mister and miss," she answered her cell.

Charlotte laughed. "I like that one. What are you doing tomorrow? I was going to see if you wanted to grab dinner. I could see what Gabriella is doing too. Maybe a girls' night?"

"Sick of the old ball and chain already?" Samantha teased.

"Doubtful. I don't think I'll ever get sick of him."

While Charlotte said the words about Rafe, Samantha was green with envy. She was so thrilled her friends were happily married, she just wished she could say the same for her and Nate.

"But that doesn't mean I just forget about my friends," Charlotte added before giggling. "I pretty much had to demand

Rafe and I have a monthly night with friends that doesn't include each other. It was kind of sweet this morning when he was stomping his foot about it."

Samantha couldn't contain her laughter. "I seriously cannot picture Rafe stomping around."

"You'd be surprised," she said coyly. "He doesn't like it when he doesn't get his way."

"Is that just a general male thing?"

"Maybe. I'm also a grump when things don't go my way, so who knows."

"Yikes. Is now not the best time to tell you I can't do a girls' night this weekend?" Samantha responded with a joke.

"Are you serious?" Charlotte groaned. "What are you doing?"

"Currently, I'm standing in Nate's living room," she said, treading lightly. Not that it made a difference. Her friend wasn't going to easily drop the subject of her current location.

Charlotte hummed. "That's interesting. You're at Nate's house. What is this, like, the fifth time in the past few months? Is this for a frequent flyer reward or something?"

Samantha was about to defend herself but Charlotte kept talking.

"Is this the same Nate who dragged you out of my wedding reception, never to be seen again that night?"

"I can explain. It—"

"And isn't this..." Charlotte interrupted her, "the same Nate we grew up with? The same Nate you swear you're only friends with?"

"Yes!" Samantha exclaimed. "Yes to all of it! It's not a big deal, I've just been visiting a bit more."

"So has he."

Samantha wouldn't survive a police interrogation. She was sweating from all of Charlotte's questioning.

"You two are seriously just friends?" Charlotte asked again.

"Yes." She was exasperated. "Nate's always been one of my best friends."

There was a brief silence, and Samantha didn't know whether Charlotte not talking was good or bad.

"I was getting on your case to make sure because..." There was the dreaded pause again.

Samantha could tell by her friend's tone she was hiding something from her. "Because what?"

"Because Nate called me yesterday and asked for my friend Simya's number. I gave it to him, not really thinking twice about it since Simya, like most of my girlfriends, has always had a thing for Nate. But with you two spending so much more time together, I want to make sure it's okay—that I'm not stepping on anyone's toes." Charlotte's bad cop routine had been dropped. Now, she was being soft and sensitive.

There was no way in hell Samantha was going to get upset—especially not with Charlotte. This was a conversation for her and Nate, no one else. But if she were honest with herself, it hurt. Nate was acting quick to ask for someone else's number. They weren't even at the courthouse to annul the marriage yet.

"It's fine," Samantha reassured her. "We both know how Nate is."

Speaking of the man, Nate walked into his apartment, shutting the door and smiling at her. He put his hand to his ear like he was one the phone, asking her who she was talking to. She mouthed, "Charlotte," then quickly got off the phone.

It was time for them to have a talk.

"WHAT DOES '*WE* both know how Nate is' imply?" Nate questioned while he got comfortable on the couch. He had a suspicion this response was going to lead to a longer discussion, and after his workday, he didn't want to stand anymore.

Instead of sitting beside him, Samantha sat in the chair

across from him. This wasn't a good sign. He was in the hot seat and had no idea what he'd done wrong.

Samantha crossed her arms. Oh yeah, this definitely wasn't looking good for him. Under the stink eye she was shooting at him, he was nervous. Nervous with no idea what crime he'd committed to turn her against him.

"Are we seeing other people?" Samantha finally broke the dooming silence.

He tilted his head. Where the hell was this conversation going? "No. Not only was it one of our rules, but I thought with everything that's transpired between us lately, it was just known we weren't seeing people."

"Uh huh." She didn't sound like she believed him, which was bullshit.

This whole conversation was irking him. Was she implying she wanted to see other people? That wasn't happening. He took a deep breath so he didn't lose his shit. "Why? Did you want to see other people?"

"No, I don't want to see other people!" she snapped.

He stared at her. "Then why are you gossiping with Charlotte about how you both know how I am? What the hell is that supposed to mean? Let alone in correlation to us seeing other people."

"Because I was talking to Charlotte and she was pushing for me to tell her why I was visiting you so much."

He cracked a smile. "Aren't newlyweds supposed to be in the honeymoon phase where they can't keep their hands off each other? Why does she have all this time to be so worried about us and your recent travel?"

"Well, I wouldn't know about the honeymoon phase, now would I?"

She stood up and started pacing. This was not how she operated. Nate had no idea what was making her so jumpy.

"I thought we were going through a honeymoon phase, at

least recently. Am I wrong on that?" Nate treaded lightly. He still had no idea what was wrong.

It was the truth about the honeymoon phase, though.

It was like the moment they'd finally indulged in sex, the world had gotten a little brighter. She was all he could think about, all he wanted. Most days, it was like she was all he needed. Having her question this was taking a step backward.

"Why did you ask for Simya's number?" she asked, pointblank.

"Simya, who lives in New York? I asked for her number because when we spoke at the wedding, she asked me for help with renovations. I don't have capacity for it right now, but I wanted to follow-up with her with my friend's contact information so he can help."

Why was she even asking about Simya?

The angry look on her face fell. She dropped her head in her hands.

"Do you plan on explaining what you meant about you and Charlotte knowing how I am *and* why Simya is even a discussion point?"

The silence stretched across the room, and Nate put two and two together. Sammy, his wife, was agreeing with their mutual friend about his past and lack of commitment. Now, she had the nerve to think he was trying to pick up their mutual friend's friend.

What the fuck was this?

Not only were they married, but everything had changed in the past six weeks. They were fooling each other if they planned to keep up the charade of "just friends."

Nate admitted to himself that Samantha's doubt in his ability to be with her cut at him. And the idea she could believe he would cheat on her...that was like a knife stabbing through his heart. The pain mixed with the anger was overwhelming.

"Samantha?" he said sternly.

She peered through her fingers to look at him. "Any chance we can pretend the past twenty minutes didn't happen?"

"Nope."

Samantha took a deep breath. "I'd like to start by saying sorry. When I was talking to Charlotte, she was asking about us, and I kept up the stupid story of how we're just friends. Then she mentioned how you asked for her friend's number and it upset me. I made the joke about how we know how you are with women, but I said it more to cover my ass and show her how not bothered I was. Then it got me questioning everything."

"Like what?" Nate crossed his arms as if they were armor over his heart. "What did you question?"

"I questioned us," she told him in a low voice.

He dropped his arms and patted the seat next to him. She bit her lip before moving from the chair.

"I need more detail."

It was paramount to hear she was on the same page as him. That she wanted to end the façade of friendship and actually give their marriage a chance. That she felt for him the way he felt for her. It was scary as hell, but they could make this work.

He was sure once all the bullshit was discussed, the easiness of being together would be back. The rules and secrets were doing more harm than good. They were more of a stopping block than anything else.

"There's been a shift since we crossed the line of friendship and..." She paused. It was like a cliffhanger, and Nate was on the edge of his seat. "And I want more. I want to be with you not as a friend, but as your partner. As your wife. But I'm scared you don't want that. Are you just waiting for our court date in two weeks to go back to your old lifestyle?"

He cupped her face in his hands and dropped his forehead against hers. "No way in hell do I want to go back to my single life. I want you, Samantha."

To drive his point home, he gave her a delicate kiss on her

lips, moving across her jaw to the soft skin behind her ear. She maneuvered her body and sat in his lap. His hands dropped to her waist, pushing her against his already hard cock.

"I will always want you," he said while he kissed her neck. "Only you, Sammy."

GOOSEBUMPS TRAVELED DOWN her body.

Nate's mouth should have been the next great wonder of the world. He tenderly kissed across her collarbone, back up her neck, landing again on her lips. When he stood, she traveled up with him. His hands explored her body just like his mouth, not letting any piece of her go untouched.

They never lost contact as he guided them from his living room to his bedroom. The sweetness in their connection was too much to ignore. Samantha didn't want to stop kissing him, almost afraid the magic they were creating would evaporate.

The backs of her knees hit the bed, and she fell ungracefully onto the mattress. It made them both giggle.

"So much for be being smooth," Nate teased as he lifted his shirt off, tossing it behind him without a care where it landed.

Samantha didn't need any prompting. Her shirt and pants came off, quickly followed by her underwear.

He gave her a lopsided grin. "You are perfection."

She sat up on the bed, scooting to the edge so she could help him tug off his boxer-briefs. "The compliment goes both ways, Nate."

Once they were both naked, he laid to her right side, kissing her sweetly while his left hand drifted all over her body. The sensation was electric and tingled everywhere. His hands on her, just like everything about him, were addictive. When his fingers grazed over her wetness, she pushed off the bed, urging him for more.

His finger slipped inside her, and his thumb brushed side to side over her sensitive nub. She wasn't sure if it was minutes or hours they were connected this way, but the build-up intensified every time he pushed harder on her clit only to be gentle again.

"Nate, please," she finally begged. "I want more."

In between kisses, he told her, "You'll get more, Sammy. You'll get whatever you want. I promise to give you everything."

It was then he rolled on top of her and pushed his cock deep inside her. His right arm was propped next to her head, holding his weight so his left hand could continue to put pressure on her clit, getting her closer and closer to climax.

When she finally came, she screamed loudly, only to have her mouth captured by his as he leaned his weight on both of his arms, pounding into her until he tightened up and orgasmed too. Afterward, he fell on top of her, both panting, out of breath.

One thing was for certain: that was the best sex of her life.

She wasn't that naïve. It wasn't just sex.

It was the first time she'd ever made love.

CHAPTER 21

WHO KNEW FALLING for someone made such a difference in life? Samantha had been on a high ever since her visit to Nate last week. She hummed on her way to the break room at work to get more coffee.

"What has you so happy at work?" Becca asked, sitting at one of the tables, flipping through an old copy of Cosmopolitan. "Is it because it's Friday?"

Huh? It hadn't even registered to Samantha that it was Friday. Just one more thing to smile about.

"Seriously, girl. You are glowing. Please, share your secrets!"

Becca's comment made her giggle. She joined her friend at the table in the break room.

"Perhaps it's because my proposal for our next interest-free credit card was approved," she said slyly, not mentioning a word about Nate.

Becca huffed. "Lies. I know this has nothing to do with a damn work proposal. What's going on? Share with me so I can be both happy and jealous about whatever has you smiling."

"Maybe I have plans this weekend I'm excited about."

She didn't.

Unless someone counted laundry, an oil change for her car, and cleaning her house exciting.

"Fine, I'll take the bait. What plans do you have?"

Samantha couldn't stop smiling. She wondered if everyone who had friends with amazing benefits felt this way. Granted, she wasn't a fan of the title, but she wasn't sure what else to call what was happening between her and Nate. Taking baby steps was probably the best option since they'd both agreed they still didn't want to tell anyone what was going on.

"Okay, no plans. I'm just in a good mood."

Becca retaliated with a stern look. "Okay, Miss Secrets. How about we have drinks next weekend?"

"Do you mind if Nate comes?" It was their last weekend together as man and wife. A couple days after, they'd meet in Vegas to get their nuptials annulled.

"Your hot as hell bestie you swear is just a friend?"

"The one and only." Samantha omitted sharing anything else. Not until they both agreed they were ready. Once they were, she was telling Becca first.

"Hell yes he can come!" she responded, wagging her eyebrows up and down.

Samantha shook her head at her friend's absurdity and went back to her workstation. When she picked up her cell, a text from Nate waited for her.

I miss the fuck out of you. Please tell me you don't have plans so we can talk tonight.

This was one more thing she was becoming obsessed with: his sweet yet snarky texts. She sent him a reply.

My only plan was to talk to you. I'll call after dinner and a shower.

He responded back about how she was a tease, which made her laugh.

Things were looking good for her and Nate. Nothing could make them take a step back at this point.

. . .

"**WHY ARE WE** leaving your bed?" Nate nagged Samantha. Since he arrived yesterday, they went to dinner, then spent all night and all morning in bed. Apparently, lunch time was when Samantha called it quits.

She sweetly pushed the strands of hair out of his face. "Because we're meeting Becca for drinks. Noah's game is on, and I thought we could all watch it and have a few beers."

He tried to pull her back to bed, but she slid away from him. "We have an hour to shower, get dressed, and meet her."

Fuck, he loved looking at Samantha. Especially when she was naked. It was a sight he would never get sick of seeing.

"I'll be amendable to this so long as I can shower with you."

"Duh," Samantha said. "Why else would it take us an hour to get dressed and meet at a bar literally five minutes from my house?"

This was reason enough to have Nate scrambling out of bed to get in the shower with her.

It turned out they were almost thirty minutes late. Nate blamed Samantha. She got ready in nothing but her underwear, and it proved to be problematic. One round led to another, and...well, now they were late.

They joined Becca at a table where she sat, playing on her phone.

"Sorry we're late," Samantha begun with an apology as she sat down. "I lost track of time getting ready, and with Nate's jet lag, I let him sleep."

Becca looked them both over with some serious doubt in her eyes. She brushed them off being late with a wave of her hand. "You're lucky all these soccer studs are here or I would have been utterly bored. I got a pitcher of Black Hammer, is that okay?"

"I haven't had that in years," Nate told her, sitting in an empty chair. "They don't sell it in New York."

"Speaking of New York," Becca said with a wide grin. "You're taking my girl away too much. I need my wingman back."

It surprised Nate to hear Sammy in a wingman capacity still, but he reminded himself how they weren't telling people about being together. To give her credit, she was the best wingman, but he wasn't sure how he felt about her residing back into that role. He glanced at her, but she was all eyes on the television, watching her brother play. For as long as he could remember, she'd been his biggest fan.

"I'm still trying to figure out why she's been visiting so much. I mean, you're a good time and all, but it's been so frequent lately. What, do you have someone with a magic dick out there for her?"

Becca was always to the point, albeit a bit crude, but it was something he liked about her.

He grinned while taking a sip of his beer. "Magic dick, huh? That's something you'd have to ask her about."

"Score!" Samantha yelled, clapping like a maniac over Noah making a goal. She turned and smiled at him. "Did you see that kick?"

"I missed it but promise to watch it on replay."

Their eyes navigated to the television to watch the playback of Noah scoring. The crowd in the bar continued to boisterously cheer.

After the noise died down, Samantha eyed him and Becca. "What were you two gabbing about?"

"It seems Becca misses you as her wingman," Nate responded with an arched eyebrow. He wasn't a fan of Becca's commentary, regardless of how true it may have been. But that was all past tense. He was hanging on the edge of his seat right now, waiting for Samantha to reassure him she wasn't going back to her old ways. He was so ready for her to deny her wingman status, he even left out telling her the funny comment about his magic dick.

Talk about a cliffhanger.

Becca nodded. "Yes, you've been acting different lately. Perhaps this is because of your many visits to New York. I need you back to flirt mode when we go out. When are you coming back to bar hop and break hearts with me?"

"You're so dramatic! I promise to hang out soon. In two weeks, we'll be back on the prowl," Samantha said with a wink.

"Fuck yeah!" Becca clapped as they both went back to watching Noah's game since halftime was over.

It was not missed on Nate how Samantha said she was going back to her old life. It left a sour taste in his mouth, and his stomach dropped. All along, he was the one who'd been living in some fantasy world while Samantha was ready to pick up right where she'd left off. She'd even put an accurate time stamp on it.

Two weeks wasn't some arbitrary number.

It was right after their marriage would be annulled.

CHAPTER 22

THERE WAS A certain smell to Las Vegas. The best way for Nate to describe it was a mix of alcohol, bad decisions, and whole bunch of what the fuck. It was all he thought about as he stood on the sidewalk of the main drag and pulled his overnight bag out of the taxi trunk. After he checked in, he waited at the bar in the Cosmopolitan, where he and Samantha had agreed to stay. Not that a stay over was even needed, but he'd booked a room either way.

Their appointment with the judge was just four hours away at one p.m. He figured since they were going through with the bullshit annulment, he would need the night to drown his sorrows. Ending things with Samantha was slowly ripping him apart.

He refused to be on a plane longer than he was in Vegas, no matter what the situation was.

His phone vibrated with a text from Samantha.

Traffic is a nightmare. Let me know the room number and I can meet you there so we can discuss our plan with the judge. I won't have time for a drink.

He chugged the remains of his beer, texted her back the suite number, and headed to the privacy of his room. As soon as he entered the room, he went to the bed and laid on his back. Time ticked away slowly until his marriage was over.

The marriage he didn't want to end.

It was all a waiting game.

Waiting for Samantha to meet him in the hotel room.

Waiting for their court appearance.

Waiting for the judge to announce their annulment was awarded.

Then...what was next?

This was on repeat in Nate's mind with no answer in sight. How in the hell were he and Sammy supposed to pretend like they weren't married? After three months of them playing a pretend version of house, how would they survive it all crashing down?

Could they survive it?

Probably not.

He wasn't being dramatic, but things had changed so significantly between them, there was no way he could go back to being only friends. Not only was he emotionally invested for more, there was no way he could forget what she looked like naked. How she moaned his name when he thrust into her. How she bit her lip when she orgasmed.

Fuck, how was he supposed to move on from her?

He dragged a pillow over his face.

The longer he was alone with his thoughts, the angrier he became at the situation he'd gotten himself into. Last weekend, when he'd been with Sammy and her friend Becca, Samantha had done nothing but admit to wanting to get back to being single. It wasn't like she'd confided in him later that she hadn't meant what she'd said to Becca. When they'd gotten back to her house, he'd fucked her against the counter in her bathroom and then they'd gone to bed.

It was he who was tied up in knots over their pending annulment, not her.

Samantha walked into the hotel suite with T-minus two hours until their required court appearance. And of course, she looked fucking stunning in her airport attire of leggings and an oversized t-shirt.

She pulled the shirt over her head, revealing the breasts he couldn't get enough of hidden behind a black bra. "You want to take a shower with me before we meet the judge?"

Her question was innocent enough. Well, innocent in the *let's fuck before we get a divorce* kind of way. For some reason this...this was where he cracked.

"Just one more time for me to fuck you before we go back to normal?" His words swiped back at her.

She took a shocked step away from the bed. "What's that supposed to mean?"

"What part? One more fuck or before we go back to normal?"

"I'm pretty sure we decided to see where this can go. I'm confused what going back to normal means now after you say something like that to me." She crossed her arms and stared him down.

He sat up, pushing the pillows away from him. "It means the last time the conversation came up about us, you told your best friend you couldn't wait to be her wingman again. You even gave the precise timestamp of our annulment."

"Are you kidding me right now?" Her voice was raised.

"Does it sound like this is a joke?" he matched her stance and crossed his arms. "It's like it's impossible for you to commit to anyone. Fuck, I was sitting right there when you told her you couldn't wait to be her wingman again. You didn't give a shit about me."

Samantha was playing with her hair like it was somehow a distraction to her. He could tell she was aggravated, but he didn't care.

"Nate, you're being ridiculous. We decided we weren't

telling anyone about us until we were sure. What did you expect of me?" Her voice was clipped.

"I'm going to repeat what you just said. You aren't sure we can work out, so what did I expect you to tell your friend. This is all bullshit. It's like I'm the only one who is fucking committed here. You can't even bail on being a fucking wingman."

The tension and conversations they'd put on hold had hit boiling point. It was impossible to stop the train wreck they were becoming. He started to pace around the room, unable to sit with all the restlessness building inside him.

"Don't you dare blame this on me." She pointed at him. "When things started to change, it was all because you couldn't sleep with anyone else. That's probably the only reason you were ready for us to start fucking around. You say I have commitment issues, but you better look in the mirror and see who actually has problems staying in a relationship."

"You have a damn husband for fuck's sake!" Nate felt like he'd roared the words. "And it's that hard for you to leave your past behind you."

She threw her hands up in despair. "You're the one who can't even bear the idea of telling people we're together, but you think you have the right to lose your shit because I followed your rule about keeping us a secret? Grow up!"

Through the yelling and pacing, they were now near the door of the hotel room. Which worked best for Nate. He needed to get away from her.

"I can't wait to get this annulment," he sneered.

She pushed him hard, and his back hit the door. "Fuck you, Nate. You are such a piece of shit. Get out of here!"

Without another word, he opened the door and walked out. The only noise was Samantha slamming the door behind him.

. . .

HER HEAD WAS still spinning. A shower and getting ready for her court appearance didn't do anything to wash away her argument with Nate. If she weren't so mad, she'd be impressed with how he'd managed to blame all the complications of their marriage on her. It took actual skill to be such an idiot. And Nate ranked high on the idiot-slash-asshole list.

She sat on the bed and shook her head.

This entire fight was because she told Becca she'd be her wingman again?

Okay, in hindsight, she could have assured Nate once they'd gotten back to her house. Told him she was just playing pretend like they had been the entire time. But how could she have gotten a word in with the way he'd devoured her as soon as they'd walked through the door?

He couldn't have been that bothered by the situation.

She needed some advice, especially since she was about to see him in court.

That was not the time to be airing dirty laundry. It would be like an episode of Judge Judy, Vegas edition.

She grabbed her phone and called Charlotte. That woman was full of advice, even when no one wanted to hear it.

"Hey girl," Charlotte answered brightly.

"Yeah, hey. So, I need some help."

"Are you trying to bake again?" Charlotte asked in a teasing tone.

Samantha rolled her eyes. Apparently if you blew up just one oven, no one forgot about it.

"No, no. This is more of a hypothetical situation," she said, mostly because no one was supposed to know what had happened between her and Nate. And just a little because she wasn't ready to admit her heart was breaking to anyone else.

Charlotte paused. "Okay. What, hypothetically speaking, is happening?"

"I have a friend who might have married someone without telling anybody—"

"Are you talking about Rafe and me?" Charlotte sounded confused. Which made sense. They had started the marriage craze first.

"No, this is another friend."

"Hmmm, okay," Charlotte agreed, but didn't sound too believing.

Samantha gathered everything she needed for court and put it in her tote. She had to leave in ten minutes and wanted to be prepared. "Anyway, this friend married someone who was such a manwhore, they made a big joke about it and couldn't wait until they got their marriage annulled."

"Wow. They weren't even willing to give it a try?"

"No, but then they slept together and feelings got involved. Things changed, at least for one person. The guy…he wanted to keep it all secretive. When he didn't get his way because of something she said at a stupid happy hour, he went all crazy town. But he's the one with commitment issues since he's never even had a girlfriend before."

"You can't crucify someone for their past relationship history. We all have a past, whether we like it or not. Do you think he could change?" Charlotte was gentle when she asked the sensitive question.

"He's slept with half the women from New York to California. It's like he only wants to commit because it works for him right now." Samantha hated the words as they left her mouth, then she realized she was giving way too much detail to not point a finger at herself. "Hypothetically anyway."

"Interesting," Charlotte's voice didn't give a single emotion away. "What is it you need help with? You know, since this is obviously not a real-life situation."

Ugh, this whole thing was so messy.

"If it was real, and she had a court appearance for the annulment, would you go through with ending the marriage?"

"Does this friend of yours want to stay married?"

"At the moment, she would love to throw her pointiest high-heel at him."

Charlotte let out a soft laugh. "Hypothetically."

"Obviously."

"Then whoever it is we're talking about needs to decide if the fight is worth it. If they love the person enough to trust change and follow their gut, that's exactly what they should do."

"That sounds awfully convoluted," Samantha whined.

"Just as convoluted as your hypothetical situation. I love you, and I'm always here for you. When you're ready to talk, let me know. And whoever this is about, remind them to think about the future. Is the risk worth it?"

They got off the phone, and Samantha wasn't any more ready to see Nate than she had been before she'd called Charlotte. In fact, she had even more to think about.

No way was this going to be solved before she got to court

CHAPTER 23

IT WAS AS if Nate had a death wish. Honest. Samantha walked into the lobby of the courtroom, and where did she find her soon-to-be ex-husband? Flirting shamelessly with another woman, who was also waiting to see the judge.

What an asshole.

Samantha glared when she sat down, but it didn't deter him. All he did was give her a lazy smile, like he didn't care if her blood was boiling. As if everything were fine. She gave him the middle finger, and he winked. It was making her regret not joining the meditation group Charlotte swore by. She needed anything to help her to stay calm.

"Samantha Nollins and Nate Haddic, the honorable Judge Shunton is ready to see you," a shorter man with a round stomach announced from the doorway.

Samantha stood up instantly and marched over to man, tapping her foot impatiently as Nate dragged himself away from the mystery woman. He met Samantha at the doorway and smiled down at her.

"Ready to get annulled?"

"Yes," she snapped. "Maybe not as ready as you are, as I see you already made a friend. Is that who you're calling once we leave?"

They walked down the hall, following the man who was going over the annulment procedures, preparing them for what to expect. Or, at least, that was what it sounded like. Not that it mattered. She and Nate weren't listening.

"Are you jealous?" Nate asked with a sly tone.

Samantha rolled her eyes. "Am I jealous of a woman you picked up in the lobby of a courthouse where people are most likely here for criminal activity? No, I am definitely not."

He shrugged again, like it was no sweat off his back. "That's right. You had no intention of making this work either way. Not that it matters, but the woman you're criticizing finally has a court appearance with the judge about a sexual harassment claim at her work. She isn't some criminal, just a woman who was asking for advice. But you already wrote it off like she was someone I was going to fuck. What little faith you have in me."

"All rise," the bailiff said when they merged to two different tables in the small courtroom. "Honorable Judge Shunton."

Once the judge sat down, everyone else followed suit. He smiled once he saw the two of them. "Ah, my favorite couple who apparently still wants an annulment. Please, do share what has happened in the past ninety days."

"May I?" Samantha asked while holding a folder. The judge prompted her to step forward with a quick movement of his hand.

"What do you have for me here?"

"These are pictures over the past ninety days for you to review."

"Thank you." The judge took the folder, and she went back to her desk.

He was quiet as he reviewed the pictures, most of which were of them smiling and having fun together.

"It seems as though," the judge pushed his glasses up his

nose, "you two were a happy couple. What happened to bring you both here today, ready to end your union?"

Samantha had a speech prepared because she was ready to call it quits. No thanks to Nate, as he didn't bring a damn thing to show the courtroom they'd tried and failed to make marriage work. It was as if he was jeopardizing the annulment on purpose.

"Your honor," Samantha gave her award-winning smile to the man, "as you can see from the pictures, we tried to make it work."

"Did we?" Nate snarked back. She took a deep breath before giving him the evil eye. Then she went back to all fake smiles with the judge.

"Trust me, we did," she said.

"Well, one of us did," Nate piped up.

She turned to him, ready to fight. "You are correct. I tried, but it was hard to do when my partner couldn't figure out what he wanted—single life or a partner."

"Priceless coming from you."

"You think I didn't try?"

"I *know* you didn't. Hence why we're here."

The judge tapped his gavel for their attention. "This is not the time to argue. If you both agree it's over, I will grant the annulment based on the interpretation of misrepresentation at time of vows. As long as you didn't consummate the marriage."

Silence fell across the courtroom.

IT WAS A question Nate should have been prepared for, but he was still surprised at hearing the words from the judge. For a second, he was annoyed he had even been asked about his sex life with Samantha. For some reason, it still felt private. Like it was their bubble, not anyone else's.

He glanced over at Samantha, who was not only blushing,

but fiddling with the papers on the desk. Fuck, how badly he wanted to go to her and let her know it was okay. To rub her back and assure her everything was going to work out for them. But he wasn't sure that was the case.

Not anymore.

They caught each other's eye, and Nate shrugged. He had no idea what else to do. This whole thing was a shit show.

He hid his laugh when he saw her stomp her foot because he wasn't responding to the judge. Laughing was sure to not only piss of the judge but dig the hole he was in with Sammy even deeper. He wasn't sure which was scarier: her or the judge.

"I expect an answer," the judge demanded.

"Could you...uh, define consummate?" Samantha asked ever so sweetly, which was again laughable to Nate. He knew the truth. She was not so sweet—especially when it came to the bedroom. Or the living room. Or the hallway. Pretty much any place available for them to fuck.

The judge was not enthused by her request. He gave her and Nate a disturbed look. "While I feel you both know the answer to this, I will give a summary. In reference to marriage, consummation is the act of sexual intercourse after a marriage is obtained. This is most relevant through Canon Law, which means if you do not consummate, you qualify for an annulment. Is this clear?"

"Does the number of times matter or does it count regardless?"

"Nate!" Samantha screeched, and the judge shook his head.

Again, the gavel tapped. "Order in this room. Under oath, did you consummate the marriage?"

SAMANTHA LIFTED HER head, tears of frustration building up inside her. How foolish they'd been to not be concerned about the aftermath of sex. And Nate had apparently decided to do a trial run of his comedy routine in front of the judicial system.

This was just great.

"Your honor, we did," Nate answered the judge.

"As I expected with all the flare the both of you brought into this courtroom. As I have explained, this means you will have to file for a divorce, not an annulment."

This wasn't how it was supposed to happen.

It might not have been reflective in all her past behavior in relationships, but she believed in marriage. There was something dark creeping over her that her first walk down the aisle had been nothing but a joke—a ninety-day probationary period she failed. If she failed with someone who was her best friend, how could she ever make a real marriage work?

"What would that entail?" Nate asked.

The judge took off his glasses and cleaned them on his robe. He put them back on, still unimpressed with Nate and Samantha.

"The fastest way would be for you to file a joint petition for divorce. This would be uncontested. As long as you complete the process accurately, the divorce could be granted as early as within ten days. I do want to set the standard, however, and say, historically, it does take longer. You can speak to the front desk for all the appropriate paperwork and required next steps."

"Thank you, sir," Nate replied while Samantha was wrapping her head around her failed marriage.

"And if I may say one more thing..." The judge kept them in the room. Not like they had a choice. Who would tell a judge no?

The elderly man continued to talk. "I think both of you know, deep down, whether a divorce is the right decision here. Typically, couples who come in here from a quick, drunk marriage don't have the love, trust, and friendship you two share. Obviously, I cannot tell you what to do next, but I do suggest truly evaluating how each of you feels about the other before taking any other action."

"Yes, your honor," Samantha and Nate mumbled at the same time.

It was like once the decision had been made for them, it wasn't what either of them wanted to do.

CHAPTER 24

FROM THE UBER to the hotel, there was no speaking between them. In fact, they'd skipped getting the divorce paperwork at the courthouse because it had all felt too real. At least it had for Samantha. She had no idea why Nate wasn't talking. Perhaps they had said too much at this point.

The noise in the hotel was loud, as it should have been on the strip, but it felt like there wasn't a sound.

It was eerie as they walked to their hotel room, neither saying a word, but she was surrounded by the noise of the judge's decision. It was a disheartening that this was the end for them. If it were a time to cue in her ability to poke fun at everything, she would have played the Boys II Men song, "End of the Road." But this was not a time for silliness. Hell, she and Nate were still fighting from before they even met with the judge, mixing in the future divorce was just too much.

Doom and gloom surrounded them.

Nate flopped in the chair in the corner of the room. Samantha sat on the bed.

An eternity that passed before Nate broke the silence.

"How did this happen?" he whispered.

"Right?"

He took a deep breath. "I'm sorry for earlier. I didn't mean it, when I said I couldn't wait for the annulment. I think the stress of this day tied in with my confusion on where we stood just didn't sit well with me. I never should have spoken to you like that. I'm sorry."

"It's okay. I didn't mean to argue with you either. Our whole dynamic has been thrown," Samantha admitted before falling back on the bed. "Three months ago, we were trashed at the alter getting married, and now look at us. What happened to us?"

"Honest? I think the rules ruined everything."

She sat up quickly. "What do you mean? The rules were there to protect us."

"And do you feel protected?"

She shook her head. Her heart had been hammered into a million little pieces. If anything, she was broken, not safe.

"I thought being best friends was going to stop us from hurting each other," Nate told her while he tapped his foot on the ground.

"Same. We were doing so great in the beginning."

Which was true. The first month or so, everything went smoothly. They got along, visited each other as planned, took loads of pictures. Something changed, though. For her anyway, the more she was around Nate pretending to be his wife, the more she thought of the reality of actually being his wife. It was far too appealing for her to be his.

The thing was, she was losing Nate as a husband.

She wasn't ready to let this ruin them as friends.

There was no way she would be able to suffer losing Nate twice.

"The past three months have been a whirlwind. We got drunk and married."

Nate nodded. "Check. Then we had some visits, but we have to admit, we toed the line a bunch."

"And you got super bitchy at one point," Samantha pointed out to him as a reminder.

"I'm pretty sure it happened more than once, but in my defense, this was my first time ever waking up with a hangover and a sexy wife. All the rules threw me."

"I am pretty sexy," she took a turn to gloat. It was well-deserved after their hearing today.

He smiled. Ugh, how she loved his smile. "You're the sexiest."

"You're not so bad yourself." She couldn't believe she was flirting back during all this madness.

He huffed. "You'll be off the market before you know it."

"Is that what you want?"

They sat in silence for a few minutes, neither admitting to how affected they were by ending their marriage.

Samantha sat down in the chair next to him. "Where did we go wrong?"

There it was.

The million-dollar question.

With no answer.

HIDING THEIR FEELINGS.

There.

In Nate's head, he was able to sum up rather quickly where they'd gone wrong.

Now, because they'd both gone leaps and bounds trying not to lose their friendship, they'd lost something even more important: a future together. Nate sat in the chair, holding Samantha's hand in his as they waited patiently. It was like they expected the judge or Charlotte to come in and dictate the way to solve this.

Fuck it.

If this was his last chance to tell Samantha the truth, if this was his last chance for a happy future, he was going for it.

He had to do what he found most uncomfortable: talk about his feelings.

"Samantha, I need you to hear me out."

She squeezed the hand she held, which he took as acknowledgment.

"Ever since we woke up married, which was hectic and crazy and confusing and—"

"Nate," Sam interrupted him, "I was there, I know."

He coughed to cover the groan at how he was messing this up already. Feelings were for the birds.

"Right, right. The point I'm making, or trying to make, is, for me, once I found out we were married, I went into panic mode."

Her brown eyes glittered with sadness. "Please don't tell me you want to rehash every wrong turn we took. I don't think I can do that. At least not today."

"All I need you to do is listen to me, okay?"

She nodded to listen, but the hesitation he saw it was like his words were going to ruin her day. Damn, he wished he was better with his words so he could make her happier. He had to make his message clear. He'd save all the sweetness for another day. Today, he had to make sure she knew, beyond all the poetic words and romantic gestures, he loved her. She was it for him.

"Okay, when I found out we were married, a piece of me was like I can't lose my best friend. But another piece of me felt relieved. Like it had finally happened. After all the years of friendship, we'd decided to up the ante and be together. Granted, it didn't happen the way either of us planned, but here we are, at the cusp of either ending the long road we took to get here or…"

Nate looked at her and smiled. He could look at her every day and never tire of seeing her. It was like all his life, he'd been waiting for the moment when he could cross the line and fall in love with this woman. For the stars to align where she'd be crazy enough to give him a chance, despite his past and their close-knit families.

"Oh shit, Nate," Samantha breathed heavily. "What is the or? You can't just stop when you get to the *or* part of the conversation."

"*Or* I can promise you, every day, I will try to be the best damn husband to you. We can figure out the semantics of where we live later, though I did buy that house already. I still have time until closing, but it would be perfect for us. What's most important right now is this: I promise to be there for you. To love and support you. To be the husband you deserve."

Nate took the hand that wasn't holding hers and wiped a tear from his face. This romance shit was no joke.

"I promise to always try to be a better man for you. I will wake up every morning grateful you are my wife. If you let me."

She cupped his face and rubbed her nose against his. "Is your *or* that we stay married?"

"Yes. I love you, Samantha. Let's *or* the hell out of marriage."

HER HEART WAS fluttering as fast as could be. After all the rules, all the games—hell, all the walking on eggshells, Nate wanted to stay married.

And she was game.

"Do you think we should date first?" Samantha was hesitant, like Nate's declaration might not be entirely thought out.

He smirked. "I think we're past dating if our next step is either divorce or marriage. I can promise to always take you on dates. It would be our first marital compromise."

His comment made her giggle. She'd always loved his humor.

"You do have a good point. But this is marriage, can we do it?"

Now, it was his turn to nod. "Yes, we can do anything together, Samantha. It's always been like that for us."

Nate moved off his chair and got down on his knees in front of her. Holy all things sexy was Nate kneeling in front of her. This was every fantasy come true. He was no prince charming—he was something even better.

He was hers.

"Samantha, I love you. I always have. Will you stay married to me?"

She threw her arms around him. "Yes!"

He pulled her off the chair to the floor and rolled on top of her.

Brushing some of the dark hair off her face, he kissed her neck. "You know, I'm getting a bit insecure here, waiting for the words from you."

"I promise to reconsider anal?" she said, her eyes twinkling with humor.

"While I appreciate it, no, that's not what I'm waiting to hear."

"You have the biggest cock I've ever seen?" Samantha was having too much fun making him sweat it out.

He bit her neck, and she laughed. "Yes, and from here on out, the only cock you will ever see. But that's not what I'm waiting for."

"Hmmm, that I promise to always support you? That I will always do my best to be the best partner to you?"

"Go on. I said more," he urged her.

"That I love you?"

"Fuck yes." His lips were on hers as soon as the words were out of her mouth.

Nate kissed and nipped her all over her face, down her neck, and across her jaw.

"Can we also promise to never let the sex get boring?" Nate's teeth bit her ear. "I mean, I doubt it would, sex with you is an entirely different experience, but let's not become one of the couples who only has sex on anniversaries and birthdays."

She did her best to unbutton his shirt. "I promise. I mean, it's like Fort Knox right now trying to get your clothes off. I promise to always want you like this. I can't imagine it any other way."

He paused, grabbing her hands. "Do you also promise to always be my best friend?"

She tipped her face up and kissed his nose. "There wasn't ever a question of that, my husband. Now, can we get these clothes off please?"

THANK FUCK FOR feelings, he thought as he sat up and quickly got rid of his clothing. He watched Samantha do the same as she still lay on the floor. When they were both naked, Nate's gaze swept over Samantha, loving every curve of her athletic frame, wanting to kiss every indent of her skin, desiring ever inch of her body.

There was no way in hell he'd ever get tired of seeing Samantha naked for him.

Without saying a word, he worshipped her body, kissing and licking every inch of skin from behind her ear down across her collarbone. He sucked and pecked from her breasts that filled his hands down to the soft skin on her ribcage.

His desire for her blazed through him as he heard each of her moans and as he felt the slight tremors of her muscles clenching around him. But to him, every inch of her was new, because this time around, she was his wife. They weren't dancing around the phrase anymore.

She was his. He was hers.

That was when something snapped in him—an animalistic

need to mark her everywhere, to make her orgasm so hard she couldn't respond, for their first time together officially acknowledging each other as husband and wife to be one she would never forget.

He moved down her body and licked her pussy like it was the only thing he would eat for days. He sucked on her clit while slipping two fingers inside her, moving fast.

"Oh shit, Nate," she cried out. "I'm so close already."

He moved his mouth, only to suck the skin on her thigh, leaving her red and marked. He went back to her wetness and ate her up, loving how good she tasted. He was addicted to her, wanting more of her even though he had her. His thumb rubbed across her clit, and he used mouth against her core while she screamed out.

The night was just getting started, he thought with a smile.

CHAPTER 25

SAMANTHA STRETCHED IN bed the next morning. When she rolled to snag a look at her husband, she smiled. After all these years—thirty, to be exact—she found love in her best friend. And in their pure spontaneous manner, they'd jumped in feet first and gotten married. Okay, so maybe that part was a bit blurry, but it worked for them.

"Why are you staring at me? We should be sleeping," Nate grumbled next to her, pulling the comforter over his head.

"Well, checkout is in an hour. Let's go grab something to eat before you go back to New York and I head home. I mean, it seems like we have a lot to figure out about schedules, where we're going to live with you staying on two coasts, how to pay bills, you know—all the married stuff."

He sat up, his hair in complete disarray. He looked at the digital clock then lay back down. "I already paid for late checkout. We have a few more hours. When is your flight?"

Not for another six hours. She snuggled back in bed with him. "I think I can make that work. But we do need to hash out everything else."

"Give me one more hour," he muttered before falling back asleep.

Samantha wasn't one of those people who could wake up then go back to sleep, but she wasn't getting out of bed. Not yet. She had no idea what their schedule was going to look like, so she stayed put in his arms.

He groaned, sitting up. "It's like I can feel you thinking. Let's get room service and talk through it."

She gave him a quick kiss before getting out of bed. "I want as many breakfast carbs as possible."

"Why are you getting out of bed?"

"To brush my teeth and put on a robe. Unless you want whoever delivers our food to see me naked," she retorted.

He grumbled something she couldn't hear.

"What was that?"

"I said put the damn robe on," he said, speaking louder.

By the time she got done her morning routine, Nate was in the bathroom ready to start his. She forgot his timing was all off from going from the east coast to the west coast. He had told her before it's once he went to bed and woke up the next day that things were off.

"Did you order breakfast already? I can handle if you want," she suggested. "I'm sure you need some coffee."

He spit out his toothpaste before answering. "Already ordered. I got you pancakes and waffles with a side of bacon."

"You're amazing."

He chuckled. "I got myself eggs and a pitcher of coffee."

"Gross, not one carb. Don't think I'm sharing," she teased.

He lifted an eyebrow. "I think I have my own ways to convince you to share with me."

"Hmmm, we shall see."

Just when she was about to drop her robe, there was a knock on the door. Damn, room service.

Nate, also in a robe, quickly grabbed some money off the dresser and went to the door. He thanked the person who delivered their food and gave them the cash. Once the person left, he pulled the tray in. She couldn't wait to demolish the pancakes. She could smell the syrup from the bathroom.

They got comfortable in bed, ready to eat and discuss the matrix that would become their married life.

"Where are we going to live, in California? You mentioned you bought the house, which is amazing, but what's the timeline for you to move?" Samantha asked before stuffing her mouth with a pancake.

Nate sipped his hot coffee. "I want to transition back home, but it will probably still take six to eight months. Long-term, we'll reside in California. We can move into our new home once we close and some of the base remodeling is done. The house has to be livable. Short-term, we'll have to continue visiting each other."

She pouted. Now that she had the happily-ever-after, she wanted a schedule that allowed her to wake up to Nate every morning.

"It's short-term," he said, giving her hand a kiss. "I know it isn't ideal, but when I come to visit, I'll make sure it's when I can stay for a week at a time. I know you have your work that requires you to be in the office, but maybe there can be some flexibility?"

"In corporate America?" She rolled her eyes. "Not likely. But I can see if I can do a week in the New York office once a month until you're fully back home."

"Perfect. Problem solved." Nate smiled at the first victory. "What's next on our agenda?"

"How will we pay bills? Separate accounts, joint accounts...?" she trailed off.

"Let's do both. We both put money into a joint account that pays bills, and the rest stays in our personal accounts. That way, no issues with money. Next?"

He was doing a wonderful job at problem solving. Here was one that was bound to throw him. "When do we have kids?"

He paused. "You're thirty, I'm thirty-one. I say in a couple years. Let's enjoy marriage first."

She high-fived him. "Deal."

"I'm not naïve. Marriage will take work and commitment, but we can do this," Nate promised. "We just have to communicate."

"Agreed. So, how do we tell our family?"

Neither of them had an immediate answer for that one.

Nate spoke first. "I'm in town next week because of Thanksgiving. We can tell them all then since we celebrate with all our families."

"I think we should tell our friends when we grab drinks the night before, though. Perhaps having them know will ease the anger of our parents freaking out," Samantha added, unsure of how everyone was going to react.

At the end of day, it didn't matter, but still.

What if their parents weren't happy?

THE FOLLOWING WEEK rolled around. After Nate got his rental car, he headed to Samantha's house. Technically, their house until they were ready to move into the house he had to work on, which made him smile. Since they left Vegas last week, they'd gotten into the routine of him FaceTiming her before she went to work, with her doing the same when she got home. The hours weren't ideal, but they'd promised each other to keep the schedule up until he moved back home.

Tired or not, his goal was for her to see how dedicated he was. He'd sent lilies to her just to make her smile. Granted, she called and gave him shit for what he wrote on the card—*Here's to a chance at anal*—but her laughter proved how much she loved the humor. He couldn't wait to see her.

The traffic was horrendous getting from the airport to her

house, but it was expected since it was the night before Thanksgiving. Everyone traveled.

He finally arrived, parked, and used his key to walk in.

"Hey, babe," Nate called out so she knew he was home.

She met him at the door with a kiss. He dropped the two bags he held and wrapped his arms around her. He was about to lift her up when she wiggled out of his grip.

"We need to leave now to be only ten minutes late to meet our friends," she reminded him, dragging him out the door.

Fuck. He wanted to see his friends, but he wanted to be alone with his wife more.

"How long do we have to stay?" he asked, climbing into the passenger seat of her car.

She shrugged. "Maybe an hour? I figured you'd be tired with how busy you've been with work, so I'll drive so you can have a drink or two before we go to bed."

"I need to fuck you before we go to bed." Nate was getting hard just thinking about her naked.

"Duh," she mocked him.

They talked about the weekend plans for the holiday and pulled up to the bar exactly ten minutes late, as Samantha had predicted. Nate grabbed her hand so they walked into the bar holding hands. When Samantha tried to drop the connection once they spotted their friends, he only held tighter.

She looked at him as he said, "Remember, we're going to *or* the fuck out of marriage. Let's go in strong."

She smiled widely, showing him how much she loved his response. "Let's do this."

They walked to their friends, and everyone stopped once they saw them together, surprised at Samantha and Nate being together. Everyone except a smiling Charlotte.

"I'm just going to rip the Band-Aid off," Samantha started the conversation as self-assured as ever. Fuck, how he loved her confidence.

"No, let me," he jumped in, not wanting her to tell the news on her own.

She shook her head no. "I've got tonight—you've got tomorrow."

"Gee, thanks," he deadpanned, even though that had been his plan all along. He would rather any negative reaction be given to him, not his Samantha. He figured the parents would take the news a tad differently than their closest friends.

"What's going on?" Gabriella asked.

Nate and Samantha looked at each other and giggled.

"Oh shit," Jason said loudly, as if he'd put two and two together before everyone else. "Another one bites the dust."

Noah didn't catch on. "Bites the dust. What are you talking about?"

Nate whispered in Samantha's ear. "Are you sure you want to tell them now?"

"Shush," she said, gripping his hand tightly.

"Why are you two whispering?" Elena asked.

They were all together. Well...except Oliver, but they hadn't seen him in years. It was time to tell the news.

"Nate and I got married in Vegas," Samantha started to share their love story with their friends, but she was interrupted as everyone screamed with excitement and applauded their union.

"Holy shit, sis." Noah came over and hugged her. "I never thought you'd ever get married, let alone to your partner in crime."

"That's probably why it works." Elena shoved him out of the way so she could have her turn to hug them.

Gabriella was still in shock. "When did this happen?"

"The night your brother and Charlotte announced they got married," Samantha admitted with a blush. "Long story short, we had to play we were married before a judge would grant us an annulment."

"Which we sucked at. We made rules to follow, but they went out the window once we started having sex," Nate added.

"Dude, my sister," Noah groaned.

Jason elbowed Noah. "How do you think I feel whenever Rafe brings up my sister?"

"Rafe, I told you to stop that." Charlotte pointed at her husband, but he only shrugged, a smile on his face. It didn't seem like he cared one way or the other.

"Anyway, we didn't get the annulment," Samantha told them.

"Thank fuck for that," Nate said, kissing her temple.

"And we're in love and married!" Samantha screeched with happiness.

All their friends were happy for them, buying shots and celebrating their love. It was when Rafe said, "I think if anyone else gets surprise married in Vegas, the parents are going to lose it."

Another reminder they still had to share the news with the people who could crush it. Nate kissed Samantha. He'd worry about that tomorrow.

IN THE MORNING, Nate and Samantha woke up in bed together. She loved having him so close to her and couldn't wait until it was a daily occurrence. The only rain on her parade was finally confiding in her parents she was married. Or, rather, Nate telling everyone.

Optimistically, she believed everyone would be thrilled, just like their friends had been last night.

But she had a feeling her parents weren't going to love that she didn't have a traditional wedding.

"Do you need Advil?" Nate asked as he walked into the bathroom in nothing but boxer-briefs. She made sure she wasn't drooling. She loved checking out Nate. When he wore minimal clothing was just a bonus. "That last round of shots Jason made us take is giving me a headache."

"I actually just pretended to take it and gave my shot to Noah," she admitted.

Nate walked back to her and used the water on her nightstand to take the medicine.

"So, it's just me who feels like shit?" he asked, lying back down.

"I had to drive," she defended. "I also didn't want a hangover when we told our families we got married."

"Smart." Nate rolled over to his side, trying to grab Samantha back to him. "Come back to bed with me."

"Nope. I'm getting ready then reading until we have to go."

"Bookworm," he teased.

"Always," Samantha said before leaving him in bed. It was time for her to get ready.

IT WAS CLOSE to three when they arrived at Charlotte and Jason's parents' house, where Thanksgiving was being held this year. Dinner started at four, but Nate wanted to have time with his friends before he dropped the marriage bomb.

Everything was going well, and now they were all seated at tables going from the kitchen to the dining room to fit everyone. Patrick, Charlotte and Jason's father, stood up to make an announcement for dinner. This was one of the traditions. Each year, dinner rotated houses, and the host always made a toast before they started to eat.

"This year, we've had much to celebrate. Our health, our family, and the surprise marriage of Charlie and Rafe."

Jason started to laugh, and Gabriella punched him in the shoulder. It would have been funny to Nate if the other surprise wedding his parents didn't know about was his.

"We are surrounded by love," Patrick continued on. "I am

thankful for all we have and excited for the years to come as our families grow. Would anyone else like to add anything?"

Typically, no one said anything else, then they would cheers, take a sip of whatever they were drinking, and start the procession to get to the food set up on a long table in the living room. This was the perfect opportunity for Nate to speak up, but for the first time, he was scared shitless at how Samantha's parents were going to react.

Jason, always the prankster, said, "Nate or Samantha, nothing comes to mind?"

Nate gave his friend the middle finger before standing up, making his mother scold him. He didn't respond. He was sure getting married and not telling anyone for three months was going to have a bigger reaction than him telling his friend to fuck off.

"I do have some news to share," Nate announced.

"Same," Samantha agreed as she stood up too, looping her arm through his.

"Oh my god, are you guys dating?" shrieked his mom.

"You could say that..." Jason was gloating behind his wine glass.

"Seriously, man, shut up," Nate swatted back.

Samantha smiled, and it calmed him down. She had that effect on him. He was ready to talk again. "We will always be dating."

"They're talking long-term." Samantha's mom fanned herself. "I never thought my little girl would ever commit."

"Could everyone stop interrupting us?" Samantha asked sweetly.

He pulled her hand to his mouth and kissed her palm. Everyone at the table awed, and that was enough reassurance for him.

"Sammy and I got married about three months ago," he told

everyone, his eyes locked with Samantha's. "We couldn't be happier and hope we have your support."

"You got married!" Both sets of parents shouted at the same time before standing up and rushing to give them hugs.

As it turned out, no one was bothered about their rush wedding. In fact, they all were happy they found love. Bottles of champagne were popped as they answered tons of questions about how they fell in love, when they got married, where they will live, the whole gambit.

It was the best Thanksgiving yet.

EPILOGUE
9 MONTHS LATER

"**WE'VE BEEN MARRIED** for a year," Samantha said while dancing on the bed. Nate watched her, enjoying all her excitement as she paraded around.

He was also on the bed, both of them naked, celebrating a year of marriage at midnight. Samantha was adamant they wake up and start their second year of marriage remembering every second, since this was unlike the night they actually tied the knot.

They decided to not have a reception the way Rafe and Charlotte did. To them, the wedding hoopla was less important than their commitment. Her parents were supportive, as were his, but mainly because they never thought either of them would get married to begin with. Since it had happened at all, they were happy.

Samantha fluffed down on the bed and smiled at Nate. "Who do you think will be next?"

"To go to Vegas and have a surprise wedding?" he joked.

"I mean, if that's how they do it, who cares? But who from the group do you think will pair off next?"

Nate answered quickly. "Not Jason. He has a strict no relationship policy."

"True and unlike us, he has no plan to break his commitment to no commitment. And definitely not Oliver. He never dates anyone," Samantha added, resting her head on Nate's shoulder. "At least that we know of."

"That leaves Elena, Gabriella, and Noah. Your brother is way too busy with soccer to give two-shits about a relationship."

"Gabriella is a chronic dater, but no one of importance ever stands out. Elena does have a boyfriend. Maybe her?"

"I thought we all hated the guy?" he reminded her.

"Hmmm, maybe a break-up is looming." She rubbed her hands together like she had a devious plan.

Nate flipped her to her back, kissing her jaw. "I think I need to distract you more often so you don't play matchmaker with our friends."

She arched into him, wanting more. "How do you plan to do that?"

He grinned into her throat. "Let's start this second year off with a bang."

While Nate and Samantha devoured each other, her phone started ringing off the hook. It was an hour later when she grabbed it and saw a text from Noah.

My career is over—I'm going home. I'll be at your house in the a.m.

If you enjoyed Nate and Samantha's story, please consider leaving a review on Amazon and Goodreads.

ACKNOWLEDGMENTS

The writing journey for me has a lot to do with all the people who support me. You all are amazing and I'm so stinking happy to say I am a writer, and it's with help from you. From family and friends, to the all the professionals who keep me on a deadline, I love you all.

First, let's seriously do a virtual hug to Monica with Word Nerd Editing! She is amazing. She is an editing boss and gives the honest feedback I need to hear. Monica – you are a queen. I hope you adore the final version.

As always, Brandi with E-Book Cover Designs, just gets me. With little detail, she created exactly what I wanted. You are such a badass and thanks for all your artistic design.

Huge shout out to Yours Truly Book Services. Ladies, you shine bright. You excel at formatting and do promotions and interviews, which is a huge help for me, an indie writer.

Every single blogger, writer, romance group owner, fan, and all the people who just love to read, you are magic. Absolute magic. Thank you for your support and sharing when you can! You are the rock in a writer's chaotic world.

My family – thanks for supporting me, even if it means I ramble on about characters you haven't met yet. #familyforever

My sweet boys – thanks for being patient with mama when on a deadline. You little men are the rainbow on the rainy day. I love you to pieces.

Christopher – you sir, are a step above the rest. Your support never goes unnoticed. I am so stinking happy we decided to do this thing called life together. Always and forever.

My Chels – there is never a time you aren't missed. I hope you're laughing at the antics of Samantha and Nate. I promise, you'll always find a little bit of you in each story I write.

ABOUT THE AUTHOR

Erin Lynne is romance writer, avid reader, and champagne drinker. She loves going on adventures with her husband and boys, whether building forts in the living room, epics game nights, or a day at a museum. Join her at www.erin-lynne.com and sign up for her newsletter (which she promises to be filled with lots of laughs and writing updates).

You can also find her:
Erin Lynne Romance Lovers Reader Group

ALSO BY ERIN LYNNE

Finding Love Series
That One Night, Book 1
The Longest Wait, Book 2

About That Series
About That Pact, Book 1
About That Rule, Book 2

Made in the USA
Middletown, DE
15 June 2023